Anonymous

Told in the Verandah

Passages in the life of Colonel Bowlong, set down by his adjutant

Anonymous

Told in the Verandah
Passages in the life of Colonel Bowlong, set down by his adjutant

ISBN/EAN: 9783337419066

Printed in Europe, USA, Canada, Australia, Japan

Cover: Foto ©Andreas Hilbeck / pixelio.de

More available books at **www.hansebooks.com**

TOLD IN THE VERANDAH:

PASSAGES IN THE LIFE OF COLONEL
BOWLONG, SET DOWN BY HIS ADJUTANT.

LONDON:

LAWRENCE & BULLEN,

16, HENRIETTA STREET, COVENT GARDEN, W.C.

1892.

LONDON :

PRINTED BY WOODFALL AND KINDER,

70 TO 76, LONG ACRE, W.C.

NOTE.

—o—

WITH one exception, the tales here collected have appeared in the *Madras Mail.* For permission to republish them I am indebted to the Editor.

CONTENTS.

—o—

THE

FIERY CROSS OF CHURRUCKPORE.

——o——

THE long Indian day had blazed itself out; a
soft breeze stirred the passion-flowers in the trellis-
work; and the clear tropical moonlight streaming
through leaf and tendril made the ends of our
cheroots glow red and dull like expiring gas-jets
subdued by electric light. It was after mess, and
we were sitting in the verandah smoking, and
talking shop.

"The best formation for repelling a converging
attack," observed Colonel Bowlong, "is a cross."

Whereupon his hearers experienced a sensation
of the happiest anticipation. The Colonel was a
perpetual source of gratification to the regiment;
whether he discoursed upon war, love, travel, or
the chase, he was never commonplace, he was
seldom prosy, but, I must add that when the
exigencies of the narrative appeared to demand
it, he was not scrupulously nice in the accuracy of
his details. Yet, in spite of this acknowledged

B

blemish, he never failed to command the sympa-
thetic, nay, the respectful attention of his audience.
The man who sat next to the speaker having
advanced some flimsy objection, based upon mere
tactical considerations, to the Colonel's proposition,
the latter proceeded to maintain his thesis by
illustration. This was all that was required, and
the interlocutor relapsed into smoke and silence.

"If any proof of the value of the crucial arrange-
ment were wanted," resumed the Colonel, "you
have it in the example of the fiery cross of Chur-
rückpore. I suppose none of you fellows have
even so much as heard of that affair, yet in '57 all
India was ringing with the story, and if it hadn't
been for the servile devotion of Simla to red tape,
the cross would be one of our established infantry
dispositions at the present day."

The Colonel paused, and called for a whiskey-
and-soda, an unfailing prelude to an anecdote.

For a few moments he remained absorbed in
thought. We waited until he had taken sufficient
time to marshal his ideas, and then plied him with
questions in order to start him.

"What sort of cross was it, Colonel? Greek,
Latin, or St. Andrew's?"

"How many men does it take to form it?"

"Has it ever been tried in action?" ·

" The cross is on the Greek model," was the reply. " It can, if necessary, be composed of only four men (but they must *be* men, mind you), one for each arm ; and it has been tried, so far as I know to the contrary, only once, and that was at Churruckpore on the famous 7th of June, 1857."

The Colonel lighted a long cheroot, and continued:—"I formed one of the arms of that cross ; old Hookerson, of the Shekawutties, was another ; Fleam, the Vet, was the third ; and Jack Wimbledon, the crack shot of Bareilly, made the fourth. I'll tell you the story if you like."

There was a responsive hum of joyful assent, and three men who had been playing pool in the adjoining room broke up their game, and stood by the door to listen.

The Colonel glanced at them complacently and proceeded:—"On the 1st of June, 1857, as every one knows, the entire Churruckpore Depôt mutinied. We four were the only officers in the station, and the rascals took the opportunity of each mother's son of us being on the sick-list, to march off to Delhi. Why they didn't shoot us, passes my comprehension. Perhaps they forgot us, or what was everybody's business was nobody's.

" We were living in Fleam's bungalow; our *pucka* Doctor had gone to the front, so we had to fall back on the Vet. Strange to say we all had game legs, which, however, seemed somehow to bring us into Fleam's proper branch of the business. John Wimbledon's right leg had been carried off by a round-shot in some fight to the northward, and he had been sent to us to pick up a little before going on to Calcutta; he had a wooden leg, it's true, but he was too weak to use it. Fleam's own thigh had been damaged by a kick from a horse. I had been chucked out of a buggy, and had sprained both knees; and old Hookerson was very dickey in the feet with gout.

"A day or two after our Johnnies went marching home, we received word that a lot of mutineers from Meerut were coming round our way. They had heard that some Sahibs had been left unexpended in Churruck, so they were making a little detour to repair the omission. This was serious news, but on the following night Hookerson received a message in cipher to say that Sir Colin Campbell had heard of our danger, and was coming up to us by forced marches. It was a race between the Highlanders and the Pandies, and we four lame men formed the winning-post. It's not often that the post takes much interest in a race, but it was very much the case on this occasion, I can tell you.

"Well, at last, authentic information reached us

that the Sepoys had beaten Sir Colin by twelve hours, and would be knocking at our garden gate the next morning; so that night, after dinner, we held a council of war and arranged our plans.

" We could not hold the house, for it was straw-roofed, and we should have been burnt like mice in a barn; we therefore resolved upon meeting them in the open. The formation selected was that of the armoured cross; the idea of the cross was mine, but the notion of the armour, I admit, was Fleam's.

" The mutineers were not expected till seven o'clock the next morning, so we had a good night's rest, and were called at five. We then had our tea and toast comfortably, and made our servants carry us into the centre of the brigade-ground in front of Fleam's bungalow; there they placed us in four long-armed Madras chairs, back to back, each at right angles to his right and left-hand man, legs up, feet outward, and a large metal dish-cover tied to each foot.

" We had rifles and revolvers, fowling-pieces and pistols, with heaps of ammunition placed handy, and upon one arm of each man's chair was a brandy peg. Our medical adviser would not allow us any more, and he was right, for it might have spoilt our figure of merit. Old Hookerson had hoisted an umbrella over his head, for he could not stand the sun, and in the centre of the cross was a hog-spear, from which floated the flag of the station commandant.

"We knew that if we could hold our own till evening we should be saved, a messenger having arrived during the night with the assurance that Sir Colin would, at all hazards, be up by sunset. The only weak point in the cross was Jack Wimbledon's wooden leg, for the servants were unable to fasten on the dish-cover; they grew nervous and shaky as the light strengthened, and they were keen to be off, so the timber was left unarmoured. Well, seven o'clock came, and we knew that the rebels were coming too, for we could hear the approaching band—so we tossed off our pegs to the health of the party and prepared for action.

"The enemy marched in to the tune of 'Annie Laurie'; they were in close column of sections, and evidently had no idea what there was in store for them. As soon as they came within range, Wimbledon opened the ball with a right and left. 'Hurrah! there go the Colonel and the Drum-Major,' he shouted, and again fired two shots in quick succession, this time bringing down the Adjutant and the Second-in-command. Upon this the column changed its direction to the left, and straightway received the contents of old Hook's heavy battery. This didn't suit them either, so they continued the wheel, and came into my focus, whereupon I let drive two barrels of my elephant-rifle right into the brown of them. Gad! such a confusion you never saw in your life; the band stopped 'Annie Laurie,' take my word, and the regiment fell back in very wide skirmishing order.

"Then they opened fire. How the bullets did ring on the Britannia metal, and send the chips flying from the chairs! but we shot ten times as steadily as they did, and we kept them at a very respectful distance. Hour followed hour with nothing to break the monotony of the fight. The enemy lacked heart and we lacked legs. The heat was killing, but the smoke kept off the sun, and we sat under a reg'lar sulphurous canopy, as the poetic sportsman calls it.

"Once, though, I felt sure they had closed with us, and had rushed the Wimbledon arm. It was about noon, and by that time they had got well round us, and were firing briskly from every side, but they were making specially heavy practice on Wimbledon. All of a sudden I got a thundering crack on the back of the head from something that came flying from the rear. 'Only my wooden

leg shot off,' shouted Wimbledon; 'the black-
guards have got my range now.' They *had* got
his range, and a few minutes later he ceased
firing.

"'Something's gone wrong with Jack,' said
Hookerson, who was on my left, and could see
him, 'I'm afraid he's done for.' So he was, and
to save the rear from a rush, I had to send every
second shot backwards over my head—fatiguing
work when kept up for several hours under a June
sun.

"At about two o'clock there came a groan from
my right; it was from the Vet. 'What's ·the
row with *you?*' I asked; and looking round I
saw poor Fleam's head hanging over the side of
his chair. He had been shot through the temples.

"I reported the casualty to old Hook, and
though he, by virtue of seniority, was in command
of the cross, I ventured to point out the necessity
of his opening a reverse fire. He told me not to
dictate to him, that he was directing the defence
and had entered the service before I was born,
&c. Nevertheless, he took up the double duty,
though he growled that to do his own work properly was as much as he could manage, without
having to keep another man's front clear; but he
was always a grumbler, was Hookerson.

" There was luckily no wind, and the smoke, as I have said, hung round us in heavy clouds, rendering it impossible for the enemy to discover how many of us were still alive, and to this I ascribe our ability to hold them at bay so long.

" I was in prize form that day and shot like Cupid. Hookerson also levelled very effectively, and did a lot of damage to the enemy before they grassed him, which luckily didn't happen till nearly the close of the day. The sun was just setting, and, as I afterwards told his widow, it must have been between half-past six and seven when I heard her lamented husband grunt. He gave just such a grunt as he used to give when he had a bad twinge of gout, only the gout made him swear too.

" ' Toe nipping you, Hookerson ? ' I asked.

" ' I've had something that will cure me of all that,' he gasped ; ' chap in yellow turban shot me, he's a marksman, notch him, or you're a dead man ;—I hand over to you—charge of the defences.—Good-bye.' And I was left alone firing right, left, rear, and centre ; pistol, revolver, smoothbore, and rifle, as fast as I could load and loose 'em. It was hard work, I can assure you. I could not do it now, but I was young then, and, moreover, I felt that upon my efforts depended the character of the new formation, to say nothing of my own life, which counted for something, for life's worth having at five-and-twenty.

"At last the enemy discovered that they had only one man to deal with, and I heard their bugles sounding the advance. I slipped my hand into the cartridge-barrel by my side, for I was determined to sell my life dearly. Gad! sir, the barrel was empty!"

The narrator paused for a moment, and then suddenly inquired, looking round the silent audience, "Did you fellows ever hear the pipes play 'Gillie Callum?'" We replied that most of us had enjoyed that harmonic treat. "That tune," said the Colonel slowly and solemnly, "makes my heart jump like a champagne-cork, and sets my blood dancing like the wine. Well, when I found that I hadn't a shot left in the locker, I put down my rifle, kicked off the dish-covers, and drew my sword. The sepoys were coming on with fixed bayonets, but they approached me cautiously, they didn't like the look of the cross, though three-fourths of its garrison were dead men. There was a moral effect about it that held 'em back a bit, and saved my life. All at once I heard the bagpipes skirling out 'Gillie Callum.' The sepoys heard it too, and halted. 'Game's won,' said I to myself, and, sheathing my sword, I lighted a cheroot. I hadn't had a smoke since the morning —too much occupied for 'baccy, you can well believe. I took it calmly enough, you'll say, but I admit that I felt glad the fight was over. I. was tired and thirsty, and there was no doubt about it that matters had been run a trifle close. It was a pity, though, I never had a shot at the chap in the yellow turban, just for the sake of old Hook.

" Well, the Highlanders came on, and the sepoys went off, and Sir Colin cantered up to the cross where the flag was still flying, cut all to ribands, though it was. He looked at it, and he looked at me in his grim way, and I could see that he was fairly puzzled.

" ' Why do you go into action in an arm-chair, sir, and where are your men ? ' he growled.

" ' I can't use my legs, Sir Colin, and I haven't got any men,' I replied.

" ' But where are the troops that fought this battle ? ' he inquired, and he waved his hand round the corpse-strewn field.

" ' In these four chairs, sir,' said I.

" It was a long time before I could make the old Chief understand how it was done, but, by George ! when he did grasp the notion, no man could have recognized the work more handsomely.

" He got me the V.C., and under the inscription
' For Valour ' Havelock had engraved : ' *In hoc
signo vinces*,'—classical scholar was Havelock.
The Governor-General, when he pinned the
decoration on my coat a year later, as I sat
in a long arm-chair in front of all the troops
in and around Delhi, was pleased to say that
the distinction had never been more gallantly
earned or more appropriately bestowed. Those
were his very words.

"Lord Canning's observations on this occasion
were endorsed by all the most experienced military
men of the day, who agreed that no feat of arms
performed during the Mutiny could for skill, pluck,
and originality, hold a candle to the fiery cross of
Churruckpore.

" And you fellows never so much as heard of it.
Such is fame ! " And the Colonel threw away his
cheroot, and rose to go.

We asked no vexatious questions as to matters
of detail : how he loaded his weapons ; what sort
of show the cross would have made in front of
artillery ; or how they saw the enemy through that
" sulphurous canopy " of smoke ; we urged no such
trivial objections ; and we sternly suppressed some
feeble jokes of our funny man about *seats* of war,
companions in *arms*, and other fatuous nonsense,

but it was whispered among us that it was a thousand pities the old gentleman's unwonted modesty
forbade him to wear his well-earned decoration,
or even to show it either to his warmest admirer,
or to his dearest friend.

THE DEMON OF THE JHOOT.

———o———

SNAPPER, our last joined, had just returned from a shooting excursion to the *Kudri Mûkh*, during which he had bagged a hind, wounded a brocket, and seen a tiger, which, from its mangy appearance, he opined to be a man-eater. On the evening of his return, the cornet's adventures formed the main subject of discussion at mess, and the extreme cunning of the man-eater having been adverted to, Colonel Bowlong, in illustration of the almost devilish ingenuity sometimes displayed by those velvet-footed ogres, told us the following singular story :—

"When I first joined the Pandours," said the Colonel, " the Deccan was ringing with the awful depredations of a tiger known throughout the country to the south of the Nerbudda as the Great Jhoot Demon. This truculent brute was the very incarnation of ravage, he rendered high-roads impassable, depopulated whole villages, and reduced formerly prosperous tracts of country to the condition of a howling wilderness; moreover, he killed every shikari, native or European, that tried to bag him. It did not matter in the least whether he was stalked on the most scientific principles, or laid in wait for with all the precautions that foresight could suggest; the result was monotonously the same—the man was always killed. But, strange to relate, this tiger was never seen in a beat; he had his lair in the most inaccessible part of the Great Jhoot, and he went on his warpath only at night. There was a singular circumstance, too, about the creature's method of killing; it was always by a heavy blow, without the action of either tooth or claw; the blood was then sucked through an orifice made over the jugular vein, and he was never known either to mangle the body or to return to it. This striped vampire would enter cottages in the dead of night,—cottages of which the door and windows had been barred and bolted —and, with a populous village around him, would silently drain the blood of an entire family. Before the bodies of his victims were cold he would have sucked the life from some unlucky being thirty miles away. How he effected an entrance into closed houses baffled conjecture; one thing alone was patent: the doors were never *forced*. The people were satisfied that this was no ordinary tiger, but a man-tiger, or a man that by eating a certain root, or by means of self-exercised enchantment, had become transformed into a wild beast. All the Bhoomkas, or tiger-charmers, of the country had tried their art upon him in vain, and it was asserted that a spirit sat upon his head and gave him warning of any danger that lay in his way. It was also affirmed that, like all man-tigers, this brute had no tail. The Demon's devastations had been going on for a great many years, and from this fact alone it was clear that he must be enormously old ; the natives declared him to be at least a hundred, and this conclusion was supported by the brute's almost supernatural cunning, which he could have acquired only by an experience far surpassing in duration any ordinary feline existence.

" As he never returned to a kill, and could not be got at by beating, the only way to obtain a shot at him was by sitting over water, and that plan offered a chance of success only in the very height of the dry season, when drinking-places were few and far between. Of course the first thing to do was to discover the pool that he frequented ; this, though difficult, was practicable, for the animal had such enormous paws, that the print identified him at once; his pug was a good deal larger than a soup-plate; it was known throughout a tract of a hundred square miles, and the sight of it sent a churchyard shudder through the whole country-side.

"About six months after I joined the Regiment, two of our subalterns had spotted the Demon's drinking-place, and, going out one night, had sat together in a tree over the water; neither of them was a bad shot, and each could claim some experience in the matter of big game; they had a powerful battery, and it was a moonlight night. Nevertheless, they were found the next day lying dead at the foot of the tree with awful fractures, and a small hole in each of their throats. One of them before he died had scrawled something with his finger on the sand, but all that we could decipher was, '*Look out for a L. . . .*' No one could interpret this satisfactorily, but the general opinion was that the warning referred, in some way or other, to a lion or a leopard. The problem, however, that remained for solution was, how a beast that could deal a blow like a mammoth inflicted a bite like a rat. But we solaced ourselves with the thought that when Culverton returned from England there would be an end of the tiger. Culverton, you know, was the man that for a bet of a thousand rupees shot a hundred tigers in one year. The best shots and the most experienced sportsmen in India were not in it with Dick Culverton; and right glad we were to hear that he was coming out before the end of his leave. I believe it was solely the report of the death of the two poor boys that brought him back, for no sooner had he arrived, than he sent men out in all directions to gather news of the Demon. In the course of a day or two word was brought that the tiger had drunk on two consecutive nights at a little pool among some rocks in the jungle, five miles off. So away went Dick, unattended, but full of confidence and with two of the best breech-loaders I ever saw. The next morning they brought him back on a litter; he was still alive, but he had sustained the usual injuries, and they were invariably fatal. He was unable to speak, but retained just enough vitality to motion for pencil and paper; the poor chap, however, could scrawl only two letters before he died. The letters were '*A. M.*' We were all much exercised as to what on earth these characters could signify; some thought that they referred to the time when the tiger came; others that they declared the Demon to be a human being, perhaps a jungle madman; but the

idea of a cannibal lunatic depopulating a whole
country-side was too wildly horrible to be generally
accepted. We soon ceased, however, to speculate
upon a mystery which could be made clear only by
powder and bullet. A deep gloom settled upon the
Regiment, for there was not a man among us who
did not love poor Dick.

" As for myself, I firmly resolved as I rode back
from his funeral to avenge him without delay. I
said nothing to anybody about my intention, for I
was then but little more than a boy, and probably
the Colonel, if it had come to his ears, would have
forbidden the attempt. But I quietly promised the
shikaris a hat-full of rupees if I got the tiger, and
sent them out to search for his next drinking-
place. Going to the rocks would have been useless, for it was known that he never came twice to
any spot where he had killed. In the meantime I
set to work to cast bullets for an old number four
elephant-rifle that formed part of my battery.
The next day, it was reported to me that the tiger
had the night before drunk at a stream eight miles
from the scene of the last tragedy. I accordingly
lost no time in setting out on my best pony to
inspect the place. It was a very wild, lonely spot,
and thoroughly *tigerish*. For a long distance, both
above and below it, the bed of the stream was dry,

but the drinking-place, which was merely a large pot-hole, still contained above a foot of water. A solitary mimosa-tree hung over the pool, but as all the men who had latterly gone after this animal had taken to trees, it occurred to me that he would naturally be on the alert for an attack from above, and as he evidently could climb like a cat I should perhaps have a better chance on the ground; so I had a square place made of leafy branches with a small hole to shoot through, and at sunset I entered the ambush. I had no one with me. A lakh of rupees would not now have bribed a native to sit up for the Demon, and as I wanted to have all the glory to myself, I did not invite any of my friends.

"The sun went down and the night came on; it was just full moon, and before the light topped the trees I grew very anxious, for where I was sitting it was too dark to see a yard in front of me, and I might have been chopped in cover without seeing my assailant. Now and again I thought I heard a stealthy footfall. What it was I could not for the life of me guess—now it was to the right, now to the left—sometimes in front of me, sometimes in rear; then the gentle patter was followed by a slight creaking noise in the branches of the neighbouring

trees ; then it ceased for a moment, and after a
little time there it was again around me as before.
Just as the full light of the moon fell upon the
stream and illuminated the surroundings, there was
an almost inaudible rustle of leaves close behind
me, and, turning on the instant, I saw a little
grey-brown paw very cautiously putting aside the
twigs of my shelter and behind the paw I could
discern two small green eyes attentively regarding
me. ' A lungoor ! ' I said to myself as it vanished
from view. A monkey ! that's what the lads and
Dick Culverton meant to tell us, and, by George !
there's mischief here.

" Moved by a sudden inspiration, for which I
cannot to this day account, I hastened from the
shelter and ascended the adjoining tree. I had
scarcely time to seat myself comfortably upon one
of the lower branches when I saw the lungoor
returning, followed by the most repulsive-looking
monster my eyes have ever beheld. You talk,
Snapper, of your tiger being mangy ; this one was
absolutely naked, nude as a nut, bald as a bottle,
not a hair anywhere—a huge, ghastly, glabrous
monstrosity, a very Caliban of tigers, as big as a
bison, and as long as a crocodile.

" As the ghastly creature crept after the monkey,
he followed the slightest curve and deviation of

his guide with the delicate alacrity of a needle under the influence of a magnet. The adroitness displayed by the tiger was suddenly converted into a subject of horrified wonder, for as the brute approached the ambush he turned his hideous face up to the moon, and I could see that his eyes were of a dull dead white, without light, intelligence, or movement. The creature was stone blind. For all that, he evidently knew, or thought he knew, what lay before him, for the saliva of anticipation was clinging to his wrinkled jaws like a mass of gleaming icicles. The monkey, when it had come within jumping distance, giving a low signal-cry, made one vigorous spring into my late shelter, alighted upon my camp-stool and sprang out again on the other side. He was instantly followed by the tiger, who fell like an avalanche upon the stool, crushing it to matchwood, and at once began to feel about on all sides for his expected victim. Now was my chance; beneath me, in the broad light of the full moon, lay the Demon of the Jhoot. I aimed steadily at a deep furrow between the huge shoulder-blades and held my breath for the shot; at that moment the keen eyes of the monkey caught sight of me, and the little animal uttered a shrill note of warning; but it was too late, my finger was upon the trigger, and I fired both barrels in quick succession. Half a pound of lead through the spine would have killed a mastodon; the Demon rolled on to his back, stretched his massive legs quivering in the air, and opened his enormous mouth in a gigantic gasp for breath. He then gave one roar, such a roar! It combined the notes of concentrated savage fury, intense physical pain, and, yes, it's a fact, the keenest *mental* agony. Before the awful sound had ceased to reverberate through the forest, the Demon of the Great Jhoot was dead.

" The action of the monkey upon the fall of his companion was remarkable. At the first sound of that trophonian cry he sprang back again into the shelter, and climbing on to the tiger's body began to search eagerly for the wound. One of the bullets had come out somewhere near the chest, and the lungoor addressed himself with feverish activity to the hopeless task of stanching the blood with twigs and leaves, at the same time making plaintive lamentation in the monkey tongue. I gave the tiger five minutes' grace, and seeing that he did not move, I descended the tree and tore down the wall of the shelter in order to have a good look at him. Upon seeing me, the monkey, applying his mouth to the tiger's ear,

strove with passionate cries to arouse the dead
beast ; failing in this he rose upon his hind-legs
and, standing upon the body, defied me to
approach. Pushing the frenzied animal aside with
the butt of my rifle, I proceeded to examine the
quarry. The bullets had done their work well; they
had entered the back close together and you could
have put your fist into the hole. I stood for some
moments gazing in mute marvel at the enormous
dimensions of the creature that I had stricken
down in a fraction of a second. What surprised me more than anything, though, was to
observe that the tiger, in addition to being
without hair or eyes, had neither tooth nor claw.
He must have been, as the natives declared he was,
nearly, if not quite, a hundred years old. The plan
of his operations was now clear enough. The
monkey was his scout. It was the monkey that
entered houses by unguarded apertures and opened
the doors. It was the monkey that discovered the
positions of the shikaris ; in short, the monkey
played the part to the tiger that the jackal does to
the lion, or the pilot-fish to the shark, and something more, for as the tiger was both toothless and
clawless it was the monkey's duty to cut the
victim's throat. 'And,' I soliloquized, as I bestowed a hearty kick upon the hideous carcase at

my feet, 'this blind machine of carnage that, left to its own unaided faculties, must long since have fallen before the rifle of the sportsman, or have starved miserably in the jungle, has been battening upon the life-blood of the young, the gallant, and the fair, a cancerous presence discharging no other function than the maintenance of one malignant life; and that this was possible was due solely to the impish perversity of an ape, a malicious midget, that, not satisfied with the puny mischief achievable by its own hands, had allowed itself to become attached in some mysterious manner to this moribund mass of death-dealing matter, supplying the monster with all that was lacking to it in sense and intelligence.' As I thought of the unspeakable evils resulting from this tremendous combination, I turned in order to brain the accursed monkey with my rifle, but the Plutonian imp had skipped."

"But, Colonel," interposed Snapper, "how do you account for the tiger following the monkey so accurately in all its windings, seeing that Stripes was stone blind?"

"Oh! that's plain enough, Snapper, plain enough, my boy," replied the Colonel, "the tiger followed Jacko *by scent*."

A SLIGHT MISTAKE.

————o————

Our Senior Major, on leaving a ball at the Residency the night before, had got into the wrong carriage, and it was not until he found himself deposited at another man's house that he discovered his mistake. "Such slips are very easily made on a dark night," observed Colonel Bowlong. "I once made a wrong shot myself that occasioned an immense deal of explanation and letter-writing before my version of the occurrence was accepted. My adventure, however, was not connected with a carriage, and the circumstances attending it were by no means of the gay and festive order. The thing happened in this way. I had been at home on leave. I had first taken six months on urgent private affairs; this I had converted into sick leave, and had got it extended to two years. Then I screwed a year's extraordinary leave, and applied for more, but the task-masters would not see it, and hounded me back to duty; so at the eleventh hour I took my passage by the P. and O. *Catamaran* and sailed for Calcutta. The voyage was uneventful until we got into the Bay of Bengal, and then we ran into the north-east monsoon. Every day the weather grew worse, and one evening, as we were going down to dinner, the skipper whispered to me that we were in for a cyclone.

" All that night the storm raged ; hour by hour the wind increased in volume ; and when the day broke great green seas were sweeping the ship from stem to stern. Not a soul dared venture on deck, and our only hope lay in the engines. At last a wave got into the engine-room, and the fires being swamped, the ship lay like a dead Leviathan exposed to the growing fury of the gale. Most of our passengers were ladies, and the scene of despair that I witnessed in the saloon when news came that the boiler-fires were extinguished, I shall, I trust, never see repeated. I was glad, however, to be able to give the poor women a little comfort. I had made the principle of these circular storms my special study, for when I was stationed at Galle I used to do a bit of yachting in a six-tonner, and many a cyclone had I avoided by my practical acquaintance with the laws that govern this particular form of atmospheric disturbance.

" I had spent the morning with the Captain assisting him with information and suggestions, the value of which he afterwards treated somewhat lightly. By comparing his observations with my own I had succeeded in fully grasping the hang of the storm that we were then struggling with; so, watch in hand, I explained to the ladies the course that the cyclone was travelling, telling them how in the northern hemisphere the path of the tempest was contrary to the direction followed by the hands of a watch. The secret is well known now, but then it was my own. I informed my listeners that I did not estimate the extent of the cyclonic area to be more than three hundred miles, and told them the rate at which I computed the storm to be travelling. ' So you see, my dear ladies,' I concluded, ' that in about half an hour we shall find ourselves at the central point of the hurricane; we shall then be in absolutely still water, when the engineers and stokers will be able to bale out the engine-room and relight their fires, while the sailors will have time afforded to them to repair damages all round, and during this interval I will, if the Captain allows it, take some of you for a little row round the vessel.'

" My prediction was fulfilled. In half an hour, or a trifle less, we were lying absolutely motionless in the very heart of the cyclone. I never in my life beheld such a scene. The sudden lull from the raving tumult of the last twenty-four hours was almost oppressive. It was about five o'clock in the afternoon, and all around us there was a dull, yellow light that might have been reflected from the abode of the lost angels. On all sides of us for the space of half a mile the water was smooth as a mill-pond, and was covered with sea-fowl of every kind; while beyond the circumference that bounded this oasis of calm, the tempest whirled in an unspeakably grand and mighty mass of billow, scud, and cloud.

" After regarding this unprecedented scene for a few moments, I hastened to the Captain and begged that I might be allowed a boat in order to take some of the ladies for an excursion across the still water, but he would not hear of it, and refused me in the most peremptory style. He asked me if I was out of my senses, and when I persisted, he was inclined to be unflattering in his language. 'The storm will be on us again in a moment,' he added, 'and besides, all hands are required to make the ship clear and tight for the next round.' Nettled and disappointed I turned away; then I did a thing that, looking back over the gulf of many years, I must admit savoured somewhat of fool-hardiness. I went to my cabin, and dressing myself in a bathing costume that I used to wear at Trouville, a perfectly correct get-up and very fashionable, I joined the ladies who had assembled on the quarter-deck for a little exercise. ' Since the boating trip is forbidden,' I said, ' I am going, without permission, for a swim,' and before the Captain could stop me I was overboard and striking out among the sea-gulls and Mother Carey's chickens. I thought I was doing rather an original thing, you know, swimming about in the centre of a cyclone, and I may fairly assume that there are few men who can point to a similar achievement.

" I was surprised to find in the course of my swim, not only birds of all kinds resting on the surface of the water, but fish and water-snakes and marine monsters floating about half submerged, and occasionally putting up their heads for air, very much as one sees fish at breathing-holes made in the ice ; sharks of enormous size were visible, but owing either to the coldness of the water or to the exhausting concussion they had undergone for many hours, they were perfectly inert, making not the slightest attempt to molest me, and I swam here and there among their ugly snouts and broad backs as unconcernedly as though they were so many mussucks in a swimming-bath; in fact, I found myself at last laying my hand quite carelessly on their cold dorsal fins. Conceiving an irresistible desire to observe the hurricane at close quarters, I swam to the very edge of the storm-skirted tarn, and there floated within two feet of the tremendous masses of rapidly eddying rain, sea-fog, and spray that, bellowing and thundering, flew past me like flocks of titanic witches speeding to a Hell-Sabbath.

" Every moment some poor storm-battered bird fluttered out of the limbo and sought shelter in the tarn, while several, as though cast by invisible hands from behind the storm-curtain, fell into the refuge stunned or dead.

" The rush and whirl so close to my eyes made me absolutely giddy, and as I turned away to gaze upon the placid lake I thought of the lines some fellow once wrote up in a public-house :—

> ' Large elements in order brought,
> And tracts of calm from tempest made.'

" I have met with something of the sort in *In Memoriam*," quietly remarked our Senior Captain.

"Ah! yes," replied the Colonel, "quite so, I knew the quotation had some connection with an inn. Well, to proceed with my adventure. All at once

I noticed a sudden movement among both birds and fish. In an instant they were on the alert, and all began to swim briskly in one particular direction; from this I knew that the centre of the storm must be shifting. A slight scud now drove in gusts across the surface of the ocean-lake, and it occurred to me that it was time to get on board again. On turning, however, to where I had a moment before seen the vessel, I found to my uneasiness that a heavy curtain of mist had descended, completely hiding the steamer from view. I swam with all my strength to the spot that I computed ought to be the ship's position, but she had vanished in the fog; there was not a sound to be heard, and not a spar to be seen!

"I confess to you that I began to grow a bit anxious. Every minute the mist deepened, until at last I was in complete darkness. Now I heard the mad shriek of the wind that told how rapidly the storm was converging upon me; the hitherto perfectly still water of my marine lagoon began to swell with the surge of the approaching billows; in five minutes the quiet pond around me would be transformed into a maddened waste of shrieking, bounding, mountainous foam. I now admitted to myself that I had been indiscreet, but I was young. Youth is reckless; and my youth was very reckless. I had, however, but little time for thought, for with a deafening reverberation the cyclone was upon me. As the giant rollers caught me in their grasp I felt coiling round my left arm what at first i took to be a water-snake, but which, in trying to disengage myself from it, I discovered to be a rope. I hauled upon it, and to my ineffable joy it did not yield; it was evidently attached to the ship, and had probably been thrown overboard for my succour. As the waves lifted me in their onset I pulled myself up hand over hand in the darkness, and in a few moments found myself upon the deck. The sailors were just battening down the companion hatchway and they allowed me to slip through before they closed the passage. Cold and dripping, I staggered, more dead than alive, to my cabin, and putting on dry clothes, threw myself on the nearest berth and fell asleep.

" When I awoke it was morning, the storm was over and a bright sun was shining. I was very hungry, and the animating clink of plates and cutlery in the adjoining saloon warned me that the stewards were laying the table for break-fast. Dressing hastily, I entered the saloon as the people were taking their seats, and I

D

never in my life made a better breakfast. When
I had finished, I looked round the table, expecting
to hear some remark upon my escapade, and to
receive congratulations upon my safe return ; but
no one addressed me, and to my intense surprise it
dawned upon me that I did not recognize a single
person present. There was a new set of stewards,
and the Captain, too, was changed. Then for the
first time I observed that I was arrayed in a suit
of check tweed ; now I had no clothes of this
pattern in my kit, and I was certainly wearing
navy-blue serge the day before. I marvelled what
could have happened to me. Was it possible that
the great peril I had so recently encountered could
have deranged my reason ? I cast my eyes down
in painful thought, my glance fell upon my plate,
and there I saw the name, not of the *Catamaran*,
but of her sister ship, the *Masula*. The truth then
flashed upon me—I had boarded the wrong ship !
It so happened that the passenger whose cabin I
had entered had been shut out at the closing of the
hatches ; he had then found shelter in a deck
cabin, and having overslept himself did not disturb
me in my unsanctioned tenancy.

" The *Masula* was homeward bound, and as no
opportunity of which I cared to take advantage
presented itself during the voyage for my shifting

to an outgoing steamer, I found myself, in the course of about three weeks, dining comfortably at No. 14, St. James's Square. Would you believe it, that when I applied for a trifling extension of leave, not only was my very reasonable application contumeliously rejected, but I was ordered to be off to India by the next steamer, and was, moreover, in the most harsh and arbitrary manner directed to explain why I had presumed to return to England without orders.

"Setting aside as the mere raving of an irresponsible clerk the injunction to return to India in such indecent haste, I applied myself to the task of trying to make the India Office understand how it had come to pass that I had missed the *Catamaran* in the Bay of Bengal, and by a pure misconception had gone on board the *Masula*. I pointed out how easily such a thing might occur at night during the hurry and confusion of a cyclone, and begged that in the foregoing circumstances a protracted term of leave might be granted me in order to enable me to recover my nervous energy, which had been subjected to so unusually severe a strain. They treated my letter, however, with the most offensive disregard. On my return from a short trip to Paris and Vienna I wrote to them again, and receiving no reply, consulted my agents as to what was to be done. They at once cautioned me that something serious might be brewing, and recommended me to drop the question of leave and to apply sharp for permission to return to India. I acted upon this suggestion, but my application was point-blank refused. I now became seriously afraid that they were going to retire me, or perhaps cashier me right away, so I thought it best to go straight to the India Office and lay my case before the Secretary of State. He listened very attentively to my story, occasionally making a note upon his blotting-pad, and when I had concluded, he said, looking at me with a peculiar expression of countenance, 'Well, Mr. Bowlong, in all my life I never heard such a remarkable adventure as the one you have just been good enough to relate to me, and I feel sure you will excuse me if, for the satisfaction of my colleagues, I find it necessary to seek some measure of confirmation of such a singular narrative. The *Catamaran* is, I believe, now at Singapore. For the present I grant you a week's extraordinary leave.'

"I suppose he telegraphed to the Captain, for in the course of a day or two I received an official letter stating that although Cornet Bowlong's explanation could not be regarded as on all points satisfactory, his account of the circumstances had, nevertheless, been accepted ; he, however, was directed to exercise sufficient discrimination on any future similar occasion, to avoid the recurrence of such an obvious irregularity. In reply I assured the India Office that I would never be guilty of a like indiscretion again, and I have scrupulously kept my word."

TIGER DAWK.

THE discourse after mess had turned upon the denizens of the merry greenwood, and one of us happening to observe that a tiger in search of prey would, in the course of a single night, cover thirty miles or so of country, Colonel Bowlong remarked :—"For a tiger, thirty or forty miles is an ordinary night's work ; I have known one do over seventy in less than six hours."

"How did you manage to follow him, Colonel ?" asked our Senior Captain.

"I didn't follow, Parkinson," was the bland reply. "I accompanied."

There was a dead silence, broken only by the rush of the soda-water that the mess-boy was pouring into the Colonel's tumbler.

"I didn't follow, I accompanied that tiger," repeated the Colonel ; "it was one of the most remarkable episodes of my life."

"May we hear about it, Colonel ?" inquired Parkinson.

The Colonel looked at his watch. "It's getting late, but the story is not a long one, and I don't mind telling it to you, for it is, perhaps, the first time that you ever heard of Master Stripes in the capacity of a carrier.

"It was just after I landed as a griffin. I was on the march to join my regiment at X., and having halted too long at Z., a small station on the road, I determined to shorten the remainder of the journey by striking across the Great Jhoot jungles, where in after years I obtained so many of my best trophies.

"I was riding a little Gulf-Arab that I had bought in Bombay, and, having sent on my kit in advance, I was working my way through the jungle by chart and compass.

"After I had ridden about twenty-five miles it began to get dark, and I was looking out for a little jungle hamlet where I intended to sleep, when I suddenly felt myself flying through the air, and turning a back somersault into the bushes.

"A tiger had sprung on my horse's neck, knocking him heels over head, and was calmly devouring him.

"How I escaped injury beats me altogether. I lay as still as a stone, thinking it best not to stir hand or foot till Master, or as it turned out to be

Mrs., Stripes had finished dinner, and started for home.

"The brute made a hearty meal off my unlucky horse, and then, having leisurely wiped her whiskers with her paws, got up, yawned, and stretched herself.

"I naturally concluded that she would now be off; not a bit of it; she had kept her cold grey eye on me all the time she was eating, and now with a purr of satisfaction she stepped over to where I was lying.

"'So I'm to be the next course,' I thought; but she was not after *entremets* and *relevées*, her little game was on a different line.

"I felt her teeth feeling down my back for a loose bit of coat to lay hold of, and in a brace of seconds she had nipped hold of me by the skirt of my shooting-jacket and had swung me over her shoulder as Réynard carries a cottager's goose, and off we went, not at a lobbing, four-mile-an-hour trot like a jackal, but at a brisk hand-gallop, varied by occasional leaps over low obstacles and sudden turns to avoid interposing trees.

"The motion was pleasant rather than otherwise, and my position was not so uncomfortable as you might suppose—it was like travelling on a narrow velvet couch resting on very supple springs. But rushing along through utter darkness on the back of a wild beast, albeit an animal you have never ridden before, soon becomes a trifle tedious; and I was thankful when the rising moon revealed the objects that we were passing.

"The journey now began to assume a real interest. We stopped for water twice, once at a pool, and once at a small stream, for the drink at the first halt was interrupted by a shot from a shikari. My companion, who escaped by a miracle, the bullet having grazed her left ear, charged with a roar of expostulation to the foot of the tree on which her assailant was seated, and for an instant I thought I was free; but she was back like lightning, and in a twinkle we were pursuing our onward course.

"While she was lapping at the second brook I managed to mix a little brandy and water in the cup of my flask, and that was all the nourishment I had till I got to X. At times my gee-gee attained a very high rate of speed. I fancy we must have been passing animals of her own species; they were not visible to me, but their neighbourhood was apparently obvious to her. Once we absolutely flew, and the pace was so severe that it took away my breath. I had no conception that any quadruped could go so fast.

We had suddenly come upon a gigantic bull-elephant standing in the middle of a little glade; the moon fell full upon him, and he loomed in his solitary grandeur like a bronze colossus of the waste."

The Colonel seemed pleased with this expression, and he paused to reward himself with a drink.

"That elephant," he continued, "presented a truly majestic spectacle, and I regretted that I was not on foot with a rifle in my hand. He scented us at once, and with trunk and tail erect, and his long curved tusks gleaming in the moonlight like ivory scimitars, he charged trumpeting straight upon the bushes through which we were trying to creep unperceived.

"Take my word for it, we put on full steam *then;* he didn't follow very far, but we kept at high speed for about a quarter of an hour when we slackened a bit, having to pick our way through a herd of sleeping bison. Did you ever hear a bison snore? I assure you the stertorous breathing of that herd made the leaves of the trees rustle.

In one place we came on a large leopard devouring a sambhur fawn. Spots snarled at us and prepared to abdicate; but we had no time to stop for refreshment, and we bounded over the quarry as if it were a log.

" Once my bearer, for no cause perceptible to me, bucked about twenty feet into the air. I think she must have come upon a snake ; I observed several very fine specimens of the hamadryad coiling among the branches of the sal-trees.

" Later on we scattered and drove into the trees a column of monkeys on the march. They were four deep just like soldiers, with a grand old white bearded ape leading the van. The way those monkeys from their place of refuge 'chattered and abused us would have made you die with laughing.

" It must have been a little past eight in the evening when we started, and we kept going till about two the next morning, when coming to some rather open and rocky ground, the tigress turned sharply to the left, cleared a large boulder like a deer, and deposited me in a spacious cave.

" The moonlight flooded the interior, and showed the floor to be littered with dry bones ; two brindled cubs were sleeping side by side in a corner on a heap of blood-stained sand.

" I saw it clearly now. I was to be utilized as infant's food. I was a plump young person, and should have afforded some very pretty picking.

" The full hideousness of my situation became at once apparent ; there I lay like a pheasant in a larder waiting till the returning appetite of my possessors prompted them to assimilate me. I say the returning appetite, for the threshold of the cave was strewn with feathers and soft down. It was clear that the little brutes had the previous evening managed to catch a peacock, and had so gorged themselves that they did not wake even to welcome their fond mamma. At any rate there was a respite for me till the morning.

"I am satisfied that the tigress from the first believed me to be dead, and I took precious good care to do nothing to disturb the conviction. She was tired with her night's work and was soon asleep, but her enormous body lay between me and the cave's mouth. Jump over her! I was too stiff with bruises to make it safe to try gymnastics.

"As day dawned, the intensity of the horror deepened. With the light came new circumstances of terror, for I observed things now that in the dim moonlight had escaped me. Among the bones that strewed the floor I noticed many that were human; the tigress was evidently in the habit of bringing home this kind of prey for the sustenance of her cubs.

"The aspect of my four-footed companions, even as they slept, was repulsively ferocious, and I began to fear that I should be tortured to death by the little demons much as a sparrow might be vivisected by a brace of clumsy kittens.

"I shuddered as the light grew stronger, for I knew that the animals might now wake at any moment, and begin the day with early breakfast.

"All at once a roar from the jungle broke upon the stillness, awakening the echoes for a mile around, and in a few moments another and a nearer roar told that the owner of that formidable *basso* was approaching the cave.

"This, then, must be the old male tiger, and from the sound of his voice he was not in the best of humours; perhaps less fortunate than his wife and weans, he had failed overnight to secure a supper.

"A third tremendous roar announced that the jungle tyrant was at hand, and as I heard the dry leaves crackle under his heavy paws, I felt that of a verity my last moment had arrived.

"But the event had been ordered otherwise. The roaring had aroused the tigress. Rising quickly, she placed herself with a low ominous growl across my recumbent form, and I could hear the gentle tapping of her tail upon the sand.

"It was now light enough for me to perceive the massive clear-cut head and shoulders of an enormous tiger in the opening of the cave. He saw me at once, and advanced with his savage eyes glaring, his lips drawn back, and his huge fangs displayed.

"But the devoted mother,—ah! how I blessed that sweet maternal instinct,—was not going to suffer her offsprings' tit-bit to be gobbled up by her lazy bully of a husband. She crouched for a moment, and then went for him like a poisoned arrow.

"They rose on their hind legs, grappled, and fell outside the cave. The tigress was active enough to whip her weight in wild-cats, and the tiger was as strong as an elephant.

"They tugged and tore at each other's throats, and used the claws of their hind paws in the feline downward drag with the most awful effect. There was no roaring, they were in deadly earnest, and fought mute.

"I have seen wild-beast fights at native courts, and have read of gladiatorial contests in the days of Imperial Rome, but to understand the full majesty and glory of animal fury worked up to the wildest pitch of frenzy, commend me to a tiger-fight in the desolation of the woods, with the conqueror's prize a living man; and to fully appreciate the more delicate points of the situation, the palm of victory should be embodied in the observer."

" Stupendously grand as was the spectacle of this magnificent contest, I could not await the catastrophe. Whichever combatant won, my fate would be the same, so I suddenly recollected that I had an engagement, and hastily slipping out of the cave, I dived into the bushes, and made the best time I could straight ahead.

" In about an hour I came to the edge of the jungle, and there found some grass-cutters belonging to the very regiment I had come to join. They told me that the station was close by, and showed me the nearest way to cantonments.

" As I went up the road I overtook the officers of my new regiment returning from parade, and introduced myself to them.

" The Adjutant inquired whether I had brought my charger.

" 'My *charger!*' I replied, 'no, thank the powers.'

" 'You have accomplished your journey from Z. very quickly, Mr. Bowlong,' said the Colonel, curiously scanning my torn coat, and generally disreputable appearance. 'In your letter to the Adjutant you said that you were to leave only yesterday.'

" ' I left Z. yesterday morning.'

" ' Then how did you travel ? '

" ' I did the first twenty-five miles on horseback, sir.'

" ' And the remainder by palanquin, I suppose ? '

" ' No, sir.' ·

" ' By cart ? '

" ' Not by cart, sir.'

" ' Then how on earth did you come ? '

" ' I did the last seventy miles or so by tiger,' said I, demurely, trying to look as though I had not performed the most striking feat of the century.

" ' By tiger ! ! ' they all exclaimed, with a chorus of incredulous laughter. ' *By tiger* ! ! ! ' And when I told them the story, bless you, I could hardly get 'em to believe it."

THE COLONEL SCOUTS.

———o———

" An Intelligence Department," observed
Colonel Bowlong one evening, " is an exceedingly
difficult concern to organize, and a still more
troublesome one to manage. Unless you have at
the head of it a man of solid judgment, all-round
experience, and consummate tact, it is bound to
prove a failure. I ran the show for Sir Hugh
Rose in his Central Indian campaign with distinguished success ; but then I dispensed with the
time-honoured practice of employing spies. I
left the beaten path there, as on most other
occasions in my life, and the results that I achieved
were stu—pendous!"

" What was your system, Sir ? " inquired
Snapper, ever zealous in pursuit of knowledge.

" Nothing elaborate about it, Snapper. I depended for my intelligence upon one person alone,
none but he knew about my plans, none but he
was allowed to execute them. I had perfect faith

E

in his loyalty, courage, and acumen, and he never failed me—that person, gentlemen, was myself."

"You did your own scouting, Colonel?"

"I did it all, and then went to my tent and wrote my report for Sir Hugh, whose admiration at what he was pleased to term my marvellous agency was enough to make me laugh in his face. I never told him *I* was the agency, he would have forbidden me to run the risk; he often said that Bowlong was worth a Brigade to him."

"Did you dress as a native, Colonel?"

"Not always. I had to do so sometimes, but my disguises were many. I once made a sketch of the enemy's position with my head in a chatty—a water-pot, you know."

"In a chatty! and where was your body, sir?"

"In the water. It was simple enough: Tantia Topi and the Rani held the fords of the Shagra-nundi river and had thrown up formidable entrenchments on the left bank. Sir Hugh wanted to know all about their position, so I went a mile or two up-stream and then took to the water with my chatty. I swam cautiously down till I could see their outlying picquets, then I slipped my head into the chatty and floated. I had brought a stylus and a plate of tin coated with wax, and as

I slowly passed the enemy's batteries I traced the lines and marked the position of the guns. I also noted how the troops were stationed. I was well satisfied with my work, and was floating on when I observed, through my peep-hole, a boat coming. It evidently contained people of consequence, for there were two red umbrellas in the stern. The boat passed close to me, and I could see the occupants; one was a young, good-looking woman, and the other a middle-aged, care-worn man. It was the Rani and Tantia Topi. "All will go well," Tantia was saying, "if they attack on the right or left, but if they go for the centre they will carry it." "Why did you put no field-guns there?" asked the Rani. "I wanted our artillery elsewhere," was the reply. "We know the tactics of these white people—it is the flank, the flank, always the flank that they work upon"—and the boat passed by. I floated on, and when I was clear of Tantia's patrols I landed and returned to camp. Sir Hugh, confidently relying, as he always did, upon my information, at once massed his troops, went straight for the centre, and carried that apparently impregnable position in seven minutes and a quarter, with the loss only of a drummer-boy's toe. The lad was nipped in the ford by one of those abominable river-crabs.

"I once had a comical adventure while swimming under a chatty. I was passing along a line of sentries, when one of them—I don't know what possessed him—took a steady shot at my covering : a regular *pot* shot, ha! ha! Well, I dived at the flash like a dabchick, and when I came up again the body of the chatty was gone, and my astonished head rose into the rim. The rascal had turned my tile into a necklace; so there was an end of my observations for that morning, and I had to dive again and swim past the line like an otter.

"I had another rather narrow escape on the banks of one of those Central Indian rivers. We had as usual been driving the enemy before us, and we believed him to be in full flight; but from certain small facts that had come under my observation I was persuaded that Tantia was about to steal a march upon us, so I left Headquarters and kept for a day or two about ten miles ahead of the army. I was on foot, and was dressed as a *fakir.* One afternoon I found myself at the bank of a river, and while debating whether I should cross at once, or wait for our advance-guard, a party of natives drew near, carrying a corpse for cremation. I sat down in order to watch their proceedings. On arriving at the ford, they placed the body half in the water and prepared to construct a pyre. They had brought a number of logs with them, and there was plenty of brushwood about. The pile was soon ready for the corpse, but just as the mourners had placed the body on the wood, a party of Mahratta Cavalry galloped down to the other bank and began fording the stream. I knew what that meant. Tantia was doubling on us, and these men were his advance-cavalry. The wily Hindu was making a dash at our communications. On seeing the sowars the villagers ran away, while I crouched behind a bush. I had no desire to be interviewed, for although I could understand the lingo, I could not speak it well enough to undergo a cross-examination, and Tantia's men had a playful way of hanging suspected spies up by the heels. I hid till they had passed, and then an idea struck me. I knew that in five minutes the entire rebel army would be crossing the ford, and it was important to know its strength. This sudden change from retreat to a forward movement might be the result of a material increase of force, and it was necessary that the fact should be made clear. In pursuance of my plan I carried the corpse to the water, and gave it a shove with my foot that sent it floating down the stream ; then, taking its place on the pyre, I covered myself with brushwood, and lay close. In about ten minutes I heard from the other bank the sound of marching men, the neighing of horses, and the roll of tumbrils; then a confused splashing in the stream, and a great hum of voices, warned me that the army was crossing, and uncommon quick they were about it. In less than half an hour they were all across, horse, foot and artillery; and I noted, as I had suspected, that the brigades were much stronger than when I had last seen them, and that the number of guns had been doubled.

"As the soldiers streamed by the pyre I could hear them remarking that they had interrupted a funeral, and some, confound their officiousness, picked up the logs that lay scattered around and threw them on the top of me. When they had all gone by I tried to extricate myself, but, gad, sirs! I was pinned—pinned like a mole in a trap —couldn't move hand or foot. Here was a nice position! The funeral party might at any moment return to complete the ceremony. Awful situation, wasn't it?—and the beggars did come too. No sooner had the last soldier disappeared in the distance than back all the mourners crept, one with a conch, another with a pot of ghee, and a third with a torch. They were evidently afraid that more troops were coming, and the thought made 'em nimble, for before you could say 'knife' the *Slokam* was chaunted, the brush-wood was ignited, and the ghee was scattered over the logs. You may imagine that I did not remain silent under this infliction. I roared at the top of my voice, reg'lar good opera-singing, I can tell you, and the mourners, thinking that a devil had entered the dear departed, flung down torch, conch and ghee-pot and made the best time they could back to the village. They had not had time to light the pyre in more than one corner, and the brushwood in that part being damp, the combustion was very slow. Still the flames made progress, and I could hear the crackling and hissing of the wood as the fire crept on. I had noticed, moreover, that the logs on which I lay were dry as tinder, and I knew that when the fire reached the centre there was an end of me, for the weight of the wood above was enough to hold me down until I was roasted. I will not attempt to describe my feelings—the horror of the situation must be sufficiently apparent to you all. But what troubled me more than the awful death that was slowly creeping up was the thought tha information, which, if conveyed to Sir Hugh Rose, might perhaps save our army from disaster, was pigeon-holed in a mass of burning timber.

"Fortune, however, had not altogether deserted me. I had perceived through the crevices of the logs that the sky above me was rapidly becoming overcast, and I now heard the sound of distant thunder. A heavy storm was brewing; if it burst in time the rain might extinguish the fire and I should have at least a momentary respite.

"But the flame had at last overcome the damp brushwood, and was making its way to the dry logs. Every minute the crackling grew louder and the smoke denser, while I could feel my surroundings becoming hotter and hotter. Hungry tongues of flame came leaping up here and there, and now and again showers of vicious sparks were tossed into the air by the rising wind. I could hardly breathe now, and I was turning deadly faint, when phit, phit, phit, came the big rain-drops, fizzle, fizzle, fizzle went the fire, and then, with a deafening roar, the tempest broke. Down came the rain in streams, in torrents, in water-spouts. I never saw such rain! the air at once turned quite cold, and I now chattered and shivered, where a moment before I had reeked and sweltered. The fire was put out in a brace of shakes, but I was still a prisoner, and I was satisfied that as soon as they could get hold of a priest to exorcise the demon, the funeral sportsmen would be at

their games again and I should be cremated right
away.

"The violence of the storm increased, and for
the space of two hours the tempest raged grandly.
Gradually a sound, of which I had hitherto taken
but little notice, began to arrest my attention;
every minute it increased in volume, and I
recognized it as the lapping of water round the
pyre. The river was rising and had already over-
flowed its banks! then a wild hope possessed me
that the tide might swell high enough to float the
pyre. Higher and closer rose the eddies, and I
could perceive the welcome water stretching far
beyond me across the land. Then joy! I felt the
cold element touch my fingers; soon it was swirling
round my neck and ears, but still the logs above
me did not move. Was I then saved from death
by fire, only to perish by drowning? No, my luck
was too good for that. With a great surge a wave
swept over my face, and I held my breath desperately; then I felt the top weight gently
removed, and I floated out into the stream surrounded by the materials that were to have reduced
me to ashes.

"On feeling myself at last free and unhurt
I was nearly mad with joy; for the first ten
minutes I shouted, plunged, and flung myself about

like a hilarious porpoise. Then I recollected that
I was the depository of intelligence, which it was
vitally important should be placed before the Chief
without delay, so I pulled myself together and
swam steadily for a mile or two down stream.
When I felt safe from the enemy's flankers I landed
and made for our camp at the double. No sooner
had Sir Hugh heard my report than the bugles were
sounding the 'fall in,' and the trumpets were
tootling 'boot and saddle,' and before nightfall we
had marched ten miles to the rear. The next
morning Tantia, thinking he had only a detachment before him, came on light-heartedly with his
entire force, and I never in all my born days saw
troops undergo such an elaborate licking as Sir
Hugh inflicted upon that army in the space of
about sixty minutes. 'It's all due to Bowlong,'
said the Chief afterwards ; 'Bowlong's worth a
brigade.'

   " One night, as Sir Hugh was sitting down to
dinner he said to me :—' Bowlong, I'd give a
thousand rupees to be able to question one of the
Rani's people.' We had not picked up a prisoner
for several days ; I had been laid up for the past
week with a bad bout of fever ; little or no information had been gathered by the patrols, and we
had altogether lost touch of the enemy. At the

General's words I rose from the table, and, pretending to recollect an engagement, left the tent.
Mounting my favourite Arab, *Morning Star*, and,
taking the syce with me, I at once started for
the front. Cantering past our outlying pickets, I
very soon found myself in hostile territory, for I
could hear sounds that plainly told me a portion
at least of the Rani's army was encamped not very
far from our advanced vedettes. It was necessary
to be cautious, so I dismounted, and stole along
a ravine that brought me almost face to face with
one of the enemy's sentries. He was leaning on
his musket and crooning an old Mahratta song.
While I was debating how to capture him I was
startled by a sound behind me that I recognized to
be the shuffling tread of a bear. I stood on one
side to let the animal go by, and, to my astonishment, I saw it pass close to the sentry, apparently
without in the least disturbing him. 'Oho!'
thought I, 'bruin is a weed in these parts, and
the sentries mind him no more than we do a
field-mouse.' My plan was formed on the instant.
I glided back to where I had left my horse, and,
taking the horse-cloth, I put it over my head and
body, and, imitating a bear as well as I could,
crept slowly up to the sentry. He did not move a
limb; in the dim starlight he mistook me for a

brown bear. I crawled nearer and nearer; and
when within reach of him I put out my arms and,
catching him by the legs, threw the astonished
warrior heavily on his back and rammed the
corner of the rug into his mouth. There was no
necessity for further violence; the man was so
startled at the unexpected attack that he swooned
right away. So taking him in my arms I bore him
down the nullah, and with my syce's assistance
carried him quickly into camp. When I reached
the General's tent, he and his staff were just
coming out to smoke.

"'Here's your prisoner, sir,' said I, saluting.

"'Bowlong,' cried Sir Hugh, 'you are unpar-
alleled!'

"I sat once rigged up as a baboon in a large
banyan-tree overhanging the Grand trunk-road
along which the enemy's army was marching to
attack our camp at Jhansi. Some of the sepoys
saw me, and pointed up, saying, 'Wah! what a
fine ape; he must be a descendant of Hanuman
himself.' In return I chattered and made the
most hideous faces imaginable at them, and when
any swell came by on an elephant, I threw a handful of small figs in his face, drawing upon myself
the choicest abuse in his vocabulary. But all
that time I was carefully noting the strength of

each battery, squadron, and battalion that filed below.

"Once, when disguised as an animal, I nearly got killed by our own men. It was a ridiculous incident, and came to pass in this way:—For some days past we had been moving over country abounding in antelope, and the creatures were so tame and unsuspecting, that a number of them had been trapped by our camp-followers. I had procured the skins of a couple of black-buck, and with a little manipulation had made myself a very effective animal disguise. My unintermitting exertions had worn me to a skeleton, my waist was like a wasp's, my arms and legs were thin as spindles, and, dressed in my skins, I passed at night for a stately old buck of but little more than the average size. We were advancing before daylight one morning in quarter-distance contiguous columns, all ready to deploy into line, for the Rani was just in front of us, retreating slowly, undetermined whether to stand or run—she had recently been getting some very hard knocks, and was a little sick at the sight of a red-coat. Between the two armies was a large herd of antelope, and as we advanced the animals moved, grazing, in front of us ; but they were much nearer to the enemy's line than they were to ours. Sir Hugh was extremely anxious to know whether the Rani was making any attempt to take up a position. The sun had not yet risen, and it was so dark that observation from our side was impossible; even if it had been daylight the clouds of dust raised by the retreating army so completely shrouded it, that we might have blundered into an ugly trap. So getting hold of my property-box, I rigged myself out as a black-buck, and covering myself with my military cloak I rode as hard as I could to the front, then, telling the mare to trot to the rear with my cloak, I dismounted, and mingled with the antelope. It was at once evident to me that the fighting Queen had had enough of the retrograde movement, and was about to make a stand. Her army had reached some low hills, and the regiments were rapidly forming line to the rear, which, of course, brought them face to face with us. By the waning starlight I could see that the Queen had a strong force of infantry and field-guns in the centre, with cavalry at the flanks, and howitzer-batteries dotted along the rear, on ground sufficiently elevated for them to fire over the line. I had seen enough, the position was a strong one, and it was time for me to get back and communicate the state of affairs to Sir Hugh. But when I turned, I saw to my intense disgust a long line of our own skirmishers advancing to the attack, and I knew that in a minute or two I should be in the centre of a storm of bullets. The enemy began to throw out light infantry on their side, and the antelope were driven gradually nearer to our people. I kept well in the centre of the herd ; the animals were growing alarmed ; the does ran this side and that, and the bucks began to make great springs in the air. I imitated them as well as I could, so as to keep up the character until I was safe behind our own lines. Nearer and nearer came our skirmishers, and I heard the bugles sound 'Commence firing.' At the first reports the antelope turned in a body to the left, and swept at lightning speed round the flank of the enemy's position, while I remained curvetting about, and expecting every instant to be shot down. At last our people came up, and some of the men caught sight of me indistinctly through the smoke. 'Shoot him, Jack,' cried one. 'Stick him, Bill,' shouted another. 'Catch him alive,' roared a third, making a grab at my horns. 'Steady, men, leave the animal alone,' thundered the Commander, and, as the line doubled past, I made a rush, dodged the supports, and, divesting myself of my outer covering under the shelter of a rock, made my way to the General and gave him an account of the enemy's position.   He at once altered the order of his attack, and won the most brilliant victory of the campaign. You may well laugh, Snapper, at the way I deceived 'em all, but, mind you, I don't for a moment pretend that it could have been done by daylight; this particular disguise was only for night-work, and you must remember that in those days I was a man of pre-eminent agility.

"When the campaign was over I brought the circumstance to the recollection of the officer who had commanded the skirmishers, and having explained matters, I told him that, humanly speaking, I had to thank him for my life.

" ' Well, do you know,' said he, ' thinking over the affair afterwards, I often had my suspicions about that antelope ; there was something to my mind not quite natural about it.'

" ' Why, what was wrong?' I asked, rather nettled, for I prided myself on the fidelity of my personations.

" ' Well, Bowlong, it was this : I had in my time seen a good many antelope one way or another, and, 'pon my word, I never, in the whole course of my experience, saw one that bounded so gracefully or that bucked so high.' "

THE COLONEL'S MIDINGHT CHARGE.

———o———

THE perfect harmony of our regiment was at one time somewhat impaired, but fortunately the discord was only for a season. The jarring element was introduced by a " doing - duty" Major, a man who prided himself upon his hard common sense and critical acumen, or, as less gifted people called it, his general "cussedness." Report said that he had been at Cambridge; it was rumoured even that he had at one time read for the Bar; he had certainly written a book, a much rarer feat in the "sixties" than in the " eighties," but " Tackle on Tactics" is now as far away in the *ewigheit* as are the manœuvres that it tended to obscure.

Towards our Colonel, Major Tackle observed a malign neutrality; but to the rest of the regiment he was actively hostile. Himself a magazine of dry fact, and gifted with more than his fair share of the dialectic faculty, he readily crushed us in debate. We certainly were not a reading regiment,

F

neither were we severely logical ; our acquaintance with *belles lettres* was meagre, and I fear that I must add that our historical knowledge was scandalously defective.

No sooner had the stranger within our gates ascertained the general weakness, than he began to harry us as a hawk might harry the tender fledgelings of a dove-cot, and with this man's presence we were afflicted during a period of six months, one week, and three days. We once, however, saw him silenced and put to rout, a circumstance that was long cherished as a golden memory.

It was a big night at mess, the 100th Hussars were dining with us, and our number-one Champagne had diffused geniality around. Even the Major was a shade less cynical than usual, and as for the Colonel, he was in topping form. We asked for the story of Churruckpore, and he gave it in his happiest manner, adding one or two interesting details that in former recitals had escaped his memory. Major Tackle, who regarded with cold suspicion everything that lay beyond the region of his own experience, and would have resigned his commission sooner than have accepted an unproved assertion as a fact, sat during the narration, glass in eye, glaring gloomily at the ceiling.

No sooner had the Colonel finished his recital, than we heard the harsh voice of the critic breaking through the hum of admiring satisfaction with which the account of that gallant feat of arms was invariably acknowledged :—

" That achievement of yours, Colonel Bowlong, is, without exception, the most remarkable episode in military history that it has ever been my fortune to hear recounted. Now, may I ask you a few questions, sir, regarding certain points in the narrative that appear to me to be, ahem ! a little obscure ? "

The tone of the Major's voice, and the peculiar smile that played over his thin lips, warned the Colonel that mischief was afoot, and he parried the attack in his own inimitable manner.

" A trifle, sir, a mere trifle. I have done better things than that, thank God ! Why, at Churruck I was assisted by three of the coolest men in the Bareilly division ; but at Delhi, at Delhi, sir, I was alone."

" And what, pray, did you do at Delhi, sir ? " inquired the Major, unsuspectingly following the herring that was being drawn across the track.

" At Delhi, when the fate of British India hung quivering in the balance, I turned the fortune of the day single-handed."

F 2

" Single-handed ! " ejaculated Tackle, with an incredulous smile, " *single-handed*, did you say ? "

" Single-handed," replied the Colonel, sturdily, "and armed only with a trumpet."

"Marvellous indeed ! it reminds one of the fall of Jericho. Your feats, Colonel, are positively Homeric," said the Major, with an air of scornful indulgence.

"I was followed by five-hundred horses, you must know," interposed the Colonel with a sly wag of the head.

"You were followed by five-hundred horse ! " exclaimed the Major triumphantly, " five-hundred is not, as a rule, you know, held to equal unity."

" Five-hundred *horses*, Major Tackle, not *horse*," replied the Colonel ; " I was followed by five-hun-dred riderless horses, with not so much as a strap to their backs."

"May we be favoured with an account of that— singularly unique exploit ? " asked the Major, add-ing under his breath : ' *Quousque tandem abutere patientia nostra ?* ' The remark, however, was lost in the general expression of eagerness to hear the tale ; upon which " The enemy," for such was the name that Tackle had earned for himself, settled himself comfortably in his chair, and screwing his eye-glass more firmly into his eye, fixed a contemptuously sceptical glance upon our commanding officer, who proceeded as follows :—

" On recovering from my injury after the affair at Churruckpore, I rejoined my old regiment, the ' King's Pandours,' then commanded by Lashem Harde, whose ruling idea was that good cavalry could do anything from furnishing a vedette to taking a man-of-war.

We formed part of the flying column sent by forced marches to capture the fort of Muzbutjak, a deuced strong place, but quite unprepared to resist an attack. In fact so notorious was the negligence of the garrison that the General had determined to take the fort by escalade.

The column advanced cautiously with the cavalry scouting just a little in advance; our leading files sighted the fort at daybreak ; the gates were open, and as all the appearances disclosed a sense of absolute security, the idea occurred to that madman Harde to rush the place with his troopers, so without waiting for orders, he took us across the open at full gallop, dismounted us at the bridge, and led us at the double into the gateway.

" But the garrison, as you will see, were not caught quite napping, and they had spotted us as soon as we emerged from cover. Between the outer and the inner gate was one of those zig-zag

approaches peculiar to Indian forts, and the regiment was soon crowded together like herrings in a
barrel.   In the rush I tumbled down, and by the
time I had picked myself up again the last man·
was disappearing round the angle.   Then came a
roar like that of a hundred-and-fifty pounder, and
when I turned the corner I saw the entire regiment
lying dead, or dying, in front of me."

The Major here snorted scornfully.

"In the inner gateway," proceeded the Colonel,
paying no heed to the interpellation, "the enemy
had posted an enormous gun, loaded with chains,
bullets, slugs, and spear-heads, and on the top of
all they had rammed down a cask of tenpenny
nails.   The iron blast, gentlemen, had simply
blown away the regiment!"

The Major here emitted a sound between a grunt
and a hiccough; his face was very red, and he
appeared to be in danger of suffocation.

"Yes, gentlemen, there lay the redoubtable
Pandour regiment, every officer and man dead as
the door-nails that studded him."

"Pray tell me, Colonel, how many men," asked
the Major, his lips quivering with suppressed indignation, "how many men, sir, do you compute
were killed by that single discharge?"

"Five-hundred, Major, five-hundred," said the

Colonel airily, and then, correcting himself, and holding up an arrestive finger, he added in a tone of lofty moral rectitude, " Stop, I am wrong, Major Tackle—I am wrong! Five-hundred was our full complement. My troop Sergeant - Major, Sam Washball, was in the base-hospital, and I, of course, was not among the victims ; the number destroyed by that discharge was four-hundred and ninety-eight."

The Colonel gazed blandly at the Major for a moment, and then resumed : " In the above circumstances I thought it best to halt a bit, so I lay down by a buttress, and waited for reinforcements. The infantry were not far behind, and in a very short space of time the fort was in our hands.

" The question then, was how to dispose of the horses, for the animals having been left outside the fort, had every one of them escaped injury. The General might have drafted them to other corps, but he would still have been a cavalry regiment short, so he froze to the nags, and applied for drafts to fill the saddles. In the meantime I was put in charge of the *manège*, and better-trained cattle you never saw. I used to exercise them by trumpet-call, sounding the calls myself. I am by no means a bad trumpeter."

The Major grinned bitterly, and glanced significantly round the table, but he failed to evoke a responsive smile from even the youngest and most irreverent stranger.

"I used to have little field-days of my own," continued the Colonel. "It was beautiful to see those animals at work ; they could perform every manœuvre in the cavalry drill-book, and a great many in the infantry, and I added one or two of my own. The Tommies called 'em 'Bowlong's babies,' and all the fellows off duty used to come over and look at us, just as though we were a circus-troupe.

"Well, after the capture of Muzbutjak, our column joined the army outside Delhi, and it was decided that my riderless command should be broken up. On the day that I received the order I went round the lines, and gave every nag a bit of carrot, for Hodson's fellows had just brought in a bandy-load, and I had begged a handful or two for my beauties. They knew there was something up, and whinnied like children. I felt like whinnying, too, but did not like to expose my weakness to the syces. I assure you I went to bed that night the saddest man in the Army, and couldn't sleep a wink for thinking of next day's parting.

"About midnight I heard a shot, then another, then a bugle went, and in half a minute earth and air shook with the roar of cannon and musketry. Bullets, round-shot, shell, and shrapnel came crashing into the camp like hail—the din was awful. The whole Delhi garrison had turned out to try once for all if they could not, by a tremendous effort, drive us from the ridge and sweep us off the face of creation. And they precious nearly succeeded; it was only my nags that saved us.

" I had no regiment to join, so, just to see what I could of the fight, I climbed up the flagstaff which stood on the spot now occupied by the memorial tower.

" The night was very dark, and I could not distinguish much of what was going on, but from the heavy firing in the direction of Subza Mundi it was evident that the attack was of a desperately determined nature. Soon I heard our bugles calling up the reserves, and in a minute or two every available man was hurrying to the front. I could now make out by the flashing of the enemies' guns that they were rapidly taking up position after position in advance of their original alignment, and it was evident that before long we should be fighting for our lives in the camp itself.

" Now, defeat at that juncture meant the rising of the Punjab, and tee-total collapse throughout India !

"A round-shot carried away the flagstaff on which I was seated, and as I rolled on the ground I resolved upon a desperate enterprise. There was no time to be lost. I mounted my horse and galloping to the lines ordered the syces to turn the horses loose. I then sounded the fall-in, and in a minute four-hundred and ninety-nine of the finest horses in India stood behind me drawn up in squadrons. I led them at a trot through the camp, made a pretty wide circuit to the right rear, cantering unperceived in the darkness round the enemy's flank, till I was well in rear of them ; I then formed line, put myself six horses' lengths in front of the centre, and advancing successively at the walk, trot, canter, and gallop, I sounded the charge—my word, sir, we did fly over the ground! You, gentlemen," turning to some of our guests, "have seen only charges made by ridden horses carrying the weight of a trooper and his accoutrements, in addition to that of their own trappings. You should see a charge without riders. It is like a stampede of mad mustangs."

The remark evoked a maniacal laugh from the Major, whose face was now turning a fine navy-blue ; but nobody heeded him, and the narrator proceeded :

"I had taught my cattle, as they advanced

to the attack, to neigh, or rather to scream ; and we swirled along, leaping, bucking, squealing, and roaring like a legion of devils. Slap-dash we burst into the very thick of the enemy. Off went their cavalry full gallop back to Delhi. The guns were silenced in a moment ; I can see now the long lank gunners, with their lighted linstocks, leaping over their pieces like harlequins in a pantomime. The infantry broke and ran, and in all directions you heard nothing but '*douro Bhai, Sheitan ke ghorè, douro douro Bhai !*'* Such a yelling skedaddle was never witnessed.

"On we went helter-skelter till we came to our own line, when we made a rapid wheel, and I found myself in front of the General and his staff. I halted the regiment for a moment just to report myself. I had only my trumpet to salute with.

" ' You glorious young fellow,' began the General, but I had no time for sweet nothings.

" ' The enemy is in full retreat, sir ; I am about to pursue,' said I, and bringing my trumpet to the recover I wheeled the regiment, and chased the flying army up the road past Ludlow Castle and the Kudsea Bagh up to the Cashmere Gate. We then gave the trembling foe three squeals of triumph and trotted leisurely home.

* " Run brother, the Devil's horses, run brother, run ! "

" When I counted the horses there wasn't one missing, but, strange to say, every one of 'em had lost all his upper front teeth ! "

" How do you account for that, Colonel ? " we asked.

" I couldn't account for it till the next day, when we found the dead sepoys lying thick as peas on the ground over which we had charged, and every man Jack of 'em had a splinter of a horse's tooth driven home into the back of his skull ! Curious, wasn't it? A glass of wine with you, Tackle." . . . But the Major's chair was vacant, its occupant, after struggling for some time with suppressed emotion, and, feeling apoplectic symptoms rapidly supervening, had gone home.

COLONEL BOWLONG'S ADVENTURES WITH THE KOH-I-NOOR.

———o———

"HAVE I ever come across a Thug?" ejaculated the Colonel in reply to a question of Snapper's, "I should rather think I have! Why, in February, '49, the whole of Thugdom between Lahore and Calcutta went for me, and I beat 'em horse, foot, and dragoons. They didn't hold a card in the game. How was it? I suppose you have all heard the story of Sir John Lawrence and the Koh-i-noor, how it came into his charge after Dhuleep Singh's capture, and how he left it in the pocket of an old drill-waistcoat, which the butler sent to the wash, first, however, taking out the piece of glass lest it might cut a hole in master's 'west.' Oh, yes, Sir John got the piece of glass back, that servant never lost anything which he thought was *absolutely* worthless. Well, the let-off gave old John such a turn that he obtained Lord Dalhousie's permission to send the stone down to Calcutta to be lodged in the Mint there, and he applied to the General Commanding the Army of Occupation to detail the most trustworthy officer in the force to take the gem down.

Sir Hugh, without hesitation, selected me for the service, and sent me to the Chief Commissioner to receive my orders. After a long look at me, and a remark as to the questionable policy of selecting so young a man for such a critical enterprise, Sir John began to enlarge upon the dangers of the road, and the prodigious value of my charge, whereupon I related one or two of my adventures, just to show him, you know, that I was not quite helpless in moments of emergency. Our conversation then took a general turn, and upon parting with me the old civilian shook me cordially by the hand, and said : — 'If any one can do it, Mr. Bowlong, I am convinced that you, sir, are the man.' It was arranged that I was to start for Calcutta that day week, and I was to manage the business according to my own ideas. Sir John had told me that the trunk road swarmed with robbers, dacoits, Thugs, and all the rest of them. The Thugs alone caused me anxiety, for a robber comes at you fair and straight, but a Thug has so many dodges and disguises that you never know when he is after you till the string is round your neck.

" The day before I was to start, my syce fell sick and died—it turned out afterwards that the Thugs had poisoned him in order that one of the fraternity might get his place. No sooner was the poor chap carried to the burning-ghaut, than first one, then another, then a third eminently respectable person of the syce persuasion came to apply for the vacant billet. They were all unusually clean, tidy, decent-looking men, and as each was provided with a sheaf of unexceptionable characters I had some difficulty in making a selection. I chose the most active of them, but, on reflecting that none had produced a reference to any person then resident in Lahore, I thought it best to secure some further guarantee of my new retainer's respectability. Accordingly I rode over to Tomlinson, who was the head of our Intelligence-department, and asked him to test the man's record. Tomlinson replied that there was an old native Police-Sergeant, he called him a darogah, living near at hand who knew every scoundrel in the Punjab, and if the policeman had nothing to say against Luxman Dass,—for that was the name of my new groom,— I might safely conclude that he was fairly immaculate. In half an hour the darogah arrived, and was ordered to interview the syce. The white-bearded veteran salaamed and withdrew, but in a moment he returned. ' The man has fled,' he said, and added calmly, ' three Thugs came in this morning from Jullunder, possibly he is one of them. I shall pursue, capture, examine, and report ; and, again saluting, he left the room. Before nightfall I got a line from Tomlinson, which ran thus :—' Your fellow is caught. He is one Drigpal, a notorious Thug, against whom we have evidence enough to hang a regiment ! ' This, I can tell you, opened my eyes pretty wide ; the Thugs had evidently got scent of my mission, and it was clear that I had now to reckon with the most formidable confederation of thieves and mur-derers in Asia. I therefore decided upon adopting a disguise, and accordingly stained my face and hands, and assumed the dress of a Pathan cossid. The great diamond was handed to me by Sir John in the presence of two secretaries, and I left Lahore the next morning an hour before gun-fire.

"My journey was uneventful till I passed the fords of the Sutlej, where my adventures began. Shortly after crossing the river, I was accosted by a Mahomedan gentleman, grandly dressed, and mounted on a fine horse, but without attendants. He addressed me most courteously in Hindustani, and, after representing the insecurity of the road between that point and Umballa, proposed that for the purpose of mutual protection we two sons of Islam should travel together. But though young in years I was too old in experience to be caught by such a very transparent device. It was altogether too thin, so I replied coldly that I preferred to travel alone. He, however, showed marked unwillingness to be shaken off, and, chatting pleasantly, continued to ride by my side. Seeing this I put on my battle-face, and producing a pistol told him that he was at liberty to ride ahead or in rear, but that if in a short five minutes he was within range of my pistol I should without more ado have a crack at him. He saw I meant mischief, so with a moral aphorism, and a polite bow, he checked his horse, and allowed me to forge ahead. When he was completely out of sight I turned sharp off the road, and took shelter in a roadside thicket, with the object of discovering whether my affable friend was on my trail. In about ten minutes he came up at a long swinging trot, at the same time keeping a wary look-out ahead. In the short space of time since we parted he had so completely altered his appearance that had it not been for his horse and trappings I should hardly have known him to be the same man. The voluminous turban had given place to a tight skull-cap; the flowing drapery had been exchanged for

G

a close-fitting *angreka;* and the ample beard and whiskers had vanished. Conceive my surprise when I recognized in the lithe, clean-shaven person that rode stealthily past me the eldest and most respectable of the three syces that had contended for my patronage the day before! I saw nothing more of my Protean friend, but I have very little doubt that he rode ahead of me all the way to Calcutta warning the entire Thug community *en route.*

"During the remainder of that day and on the following, I observed nothing more disquieting than a line of loaded camels and an occasional hackery, but early on the third morning, as I was riding along in the uncertain light of the false dawn, my horse shied violently at an object lying in the road. As nothing would induce him to pass the obstruction I dismounted and found the cause of his terror to be a venerable old man, who was lying bleeding from many wounds. In reply to my questions he stated that he had been reduced to his present sad condition by a band of budmashes, who, after maltreating him in this fashion, had robbed him of a few copper coins that he carried in his waistcloth, and had left him on the road to die. It would have been sheer inhumanity to allow the old fellow to bleed to death for

want of a little attention, so I carried him to
the side of the road, bound up his wounds, and
gave him some water, which I procured from a
neighbouring pool; and having done this I felt
that I could with a clear conscience commit him
to the charge of the first person that passed by.
But when the sun rose not a soul was in sight,
and I waited impatiently hour after hour for the
appearance of a wayfarer; noon came, and the
sun began to decline, and my patient was still
upon my hands.

"It was impossible for me to loiter much longer,
and I was beginning to accept the necessity of
leaving the old man to the chances of war, when a
beautiful young woman came along the road. She
was sobbing bitterly; her fine eyes were dim with
tears; her raven tresses hung down her shapely
back, her dress was picturesquely dishevelled, and
she kept uttering in a low melodious tone the name,
'Ramdeo.' The sufferer faintly signed to me to
summon the maiden. On beholding the old man
the girl gave a cry of joy, and, running up to him,
threw herself on her knees by his side; then, taking
his hands in hers, she cried :—'Oh, my father,
what barbarian has maltreated you thus? When
you came not home last night I feared for you,
but when the morning dawned, and you were still

away, I said, alas! he is dead, and I have found you, found you.' When the first burst of the girl's emotion was over, I told her that I must be making my way onward, and proceeded to untether my horse preparatory to a start. But she eagerly represented how utterly it was beyond her unassisted power to get the wounded man home, and earnestly begged that I would help her to convey him to his cottage, which was but a mile away. She pleaded so piteously, and presented a picture of such perfect helplessness, that I had not the heart to leave her and the possibly dying man by themselves on that solitary road. So, leading my horse with one hand and supporting the feeble steps of old Ramdeo with the other, the girl assisting as well as she could, I walked slowly in the direction where I was told lay their hut. The distance to the domicile, however, was nearer three miles than one, and our progress was so slow, and our halts were so frequent, owing to the incessant attacks of faintness which overcame the invalid, that it was past sunset before we reached the little homestead. That night there was little or no moon, and to attempt to get any further on my journey till the next morning was out of the question, so I yielded to the cordial invitation of father and daughter to accept their modest hospitality for the night.

They provided food and shelter for my horse, and made me share their simple meal of wheaten cakes and dall. After a cheroot I grew drowsy, and throwing myself down in a corner I wished my kind entertainers good night, and in a moment was asleep.

" I don't know how long I had slumbered, when I dreamt that I was walking through a magnificent tropical forest, admiring the beautiful vegetation, and the striking effect of the sunlight glancing through the interlaced branches; when, all at once, to my extreme consternation, I saw, swinging down from the topmost boughs of a tall banian-tree, the baleful head of an enormous python. In vain I tried to evade the darting horror, quick as lightning it followed every movement that I made, and in a moment the hideous reptile had thrown a coil round my arms, and another round my neck. Struggle as I would I could not free myself from its folds. I felt the constriction on my windpipe growing every instant more oppressive, and in one last frantic effort for freedom I awoke—awoke to find my charming hostess pinioning my arms, while my venerable host was drawing the fatal *phansi*, or Thug's noose, with all his force around my throttle! Most fortunately for me, the old rascal's self-inflicted wounds had weakened him beyond his calculation ; had he been able to bring an ounce more power to bear upon the slip-knot I should have been strangled before I could wake. Even as it was I had to employ my utmost exertions to shake myself free. When at last I got upon my legs I reeled and fell against the wall. I had undoubtedly been drugged at my dinner, but my great natural vitality just sufficed to overpower the poison, and I was sufficiently master of my actions to be able to draw a pistol and drive a bullet through the old ruffian's heart. The girl, seeing that their attempt had failed, slipped noiselessly out of the house and vanished in the darkness.

Weak and tottering as I was from the effects of the drug I made no attempt to resume my journey till late the next morning, and even then I did not find myself equal to a ride of more than ten miles ; indeed, it was several days before all trace of the poison left my system. It was fortunate for me that during this interval of depression there occurred nothing calling for any unusual mental or physical exertion. Another bit of excitement, however, was soon to follow.

"At the close of a long day's march I had arrived at the bank of a broad river. The stream, having been swollen by heavy freshets from the hills, was in full flood, and to cross it that night was impossible; so, lighting a fire, I cooked my meal Indian fashion, and prepared to bivouac under a tree. As I was drawing my cloak around me preparatory to bye-o, two sepoys tramped up and, after a long look at the river, determined not to try the ford. Seeing me camping under the tree they asked permission to halt by my fire, and leave being given they began to cook their dinner. They were frank, cheery fellows, and one of them wore the Gwalior Star. They told me they belonged to the 170th Bengal Infantry, and having taken part in all the engagements of the late campaign were now going home on furlough. They offered me a cheroot, and some tempting-looking sweetmeats which they said they had bought that morning, but after my lesson in the hut it was my rule to accept no article of consumption from a stranger, even though he wore Her Majesty's uniform, and was distinguished by a military decoration. My new companions were in no degree offended by my refusal, and, after some further friendly remarks, betook themselves to rest; they were evidently dog-tired and were soon fast asleep.

As I lay smoking beside them I thought over all that they had told me, and I suddenly remembered that the 170th Regiment had been present neither at Guzerat nor at Chillianwallah, and these sepoys had talked fluently about the gallant conduct of their corps in each of these actions. The more I sifted their story the more I discovered it to contain statements not only inaccurate, but impossible. My suspicions were now actively aroused, and observing that in choosing their positions for the night they had placed themselves one on each side of me I adopted such measures of precaution as the circumstances allowed. I quietly exchanged coverings with the man lying nearest to me, and shifted my position so as to leave him in the centre and myself on the flank; then, cocking both my pistols, I lay watchful as a weasel awaiting the result. At about three o'clock in the morning the man who slept furthest off arose, and gliding noiselessly across to where I was lying, placed his hand gently on my head, and hissed low in Hindustani : 'It is time.'

" ' Good,' I replied with a yawn and a stretch.

" ' Well, brother, rise and help,' he rejoined.

" ' I am too tired, do it yourself,' I grunted, and, pretending to be overpowered with fatigue, I turned heavily on my side and began to snore.

" ' Slothful pig,' he growled, ' I will report thee to the Guru.'

He then left me snoring vigorously, and cautiously approached his comrade, who, covered from head to foot by my cloak, occupied my former relative position. My back was to the pair, and I did not see what was going on till I heard a horrible gurgling noise, and, turning, I beheld the man who had been speaking to me in the act of drawing a noose to the utmost stretch of tension round his unfortunate companion's neck. I need not say that I made no effort to interfere with this act of truly poetic justice. In four or five minutes the strangler slackened the strain, and finding that his prey was quite dead, he removed his knee from the victim's chest, and threw off the covering preparatory to rifling the body. The starlight which had not been bright enough to reveal his comrade's features was just sufficiently clear to throw a glint on the bright buttons of the uniform. Appalled at his mistake, the murderer turned towards me as though to satisfy himself as to my identity, but only to see me covering him with a long cavalry-pistol.

"In a second he was grovelling before me on his face, crying :—' *Amán Amán !* '*

" ' Mercy to a *Phansigar !* ' I cried, ' I would as soon show mercy to a crocodile. But,' I continued, ' I will give you a chance — carry

* Mercy, mercy !

that body to the river, and swim across with
it, or I drop you dead.' You see I knew that
in the morning people would be arriving at the
ford, and I did not want to be subjected to the
cross-examination of the police when the body
was discovered. The Thug was not slow in accepting my conditions. Springing to his feet he
dragged his dead companion to the water, and
precipitately committed himself and his ghastly
convoy to the current. So long as he was within
easy shot of the bank he towed the corpse con-
scientiously; but when he thought himself out of
range he yelled an obscene defiance, and allowed
the body to go drifting down the stream. He then
struck out with might and main for the opposite
bank, which, at the pace the river was flowing, I
knew it to be a million to one against his ever
reaching. I then felt that I might indulge in a
little sleep. When I awoke the sun was high, and
the river having resumed its normal condition the
ford was practicable. About midstream, a little to
the right of the ford, an uprooted tree had been
washed against a sandbank : a number of crows
and a vulture were busy among the branches ; and
a nearer view enabled me to recognize as the
object of their solicitude the man who had so
readily taken to the water a few hours before.

"A day or two after this occurrence I again turned the tables upon one of these human serpents in a manner that he found both startling and disastrous. I was sleeping in a village serai, of which the only other occupant was a wretched-looking beggar, who lay perfectly still, wrapped up in a bundle of squalid rags. The night was intensely hot, and both of us had placed a lotah of drinking water by the side of our sleeping mats. Although I had no reason to suspect my fellow-lodger of sinister designs, I nevertheless adopted the simple precaution of placing a thin piece of muslin on the surface of the water intended for my drinking. Waking in the middle of the night, parched with thirst, I struck a match, and carefully examined the contents of my lotah. The muslin was still floating on the water, but it had intercepted a quantity of fine brown powder that most certainly was not there when I went to sleep.

"I stepped across to where the beggar was lying, and, having satisfied myself that he was not awake, I took the liberty of examining the contents of an old deer-skin bag on which one of his lean brown arms was resting. Among a variety of nondescript articles I observed a long narrow handkerchief of faded yellow silk, it was weighted with a .bullet at one end, and was stained with blood. I noticed also a folded leaf containing the remains of the preparation that had been so considerately added to my beverage while I slept. It was clear that the man before me was a Thug poisoner, and I thought it no sin therefore to return the attention that he had paid me, by transferring the powder from my lotah to his, but without the intervention of the muslin rag.

"Early the next morning I was aroused by a series of shrill, yelping cries, and I beheld the pseudo-mendicant staggering wildly about, grasping at the walls for support, and clutching at imaginary substances in the air. As he reeled around in drunken frenzy he at one moment laughed maniacally, nodded his head gaily, and clapped his hands, and the next he broke into loud lamentations, foamed at the mouth, and made the air around him thick with malediction. It was evident that he was under the maddening influence of datura. I never saw a fellow so completely off the handle in my life. Bedlam was a patch upon him; but I couldn't wait to watch his vagaries, for I was afraid that his yells would rouse the village, and I should be seized as a poisoner, so I lost no time in mounting my nag, and as I cantered away the vociferations of my would-be murderer grew fainter and fainter in the distance.

" A day or two afterwards I entered, as I afterwards learnt, the very heart and focus of the great Thug system. My route lay in close vicinity to the gloomy jungles of Jabri, in the depths of which was situated that foul old temple of black stone where the Jamaldevi Thugs worship their goddess, with bloody rites and lascivious incantations. Within a few miles of me were the notorious Gaurhari caves, where Sleeman discovered deep graves containing murdered people buried by fifties, one above the other, the head of one at the feet of the next, in the approved Thug fashion. Little did I know when I halted at the roadside for the night that I was about to sleep within a furlong of the gruesome grove of Kali, the most notorious *Bêl*, or strangling-place, in Oude.

" I had tethered and fed my horse, eaten my dinner, and made myself snug for the night, when I heard a sort of banshee wail coming from the road, and shortly after there appeared what, in the uncertain light of the fire, seemed to be a little East-Indian lad, shabbily dressed in clothes of the nondescript European fashion adopted ·in those days by the families of soldiers. He told me in broken Hindustani that

he had fallen from a baggage-waggon accompany-
ing a detachment of British troops on the march
to Lucknow. The fall, he said, had stunned
him, and when he recovered his senses the detachment was out of sight. Would I give him a little
food, and allow him to lie for an hour by my fire?
I of course assented, and gave him the remains of
my dinner. He munched my chupatties, sitting
the while in sullen silence with his back turned
towards me. He then got up and said that it was
time for him to proceed on his journey. Wishing
me good-night he offered me a rose, saying:—' Take,
good rose, fine smellings,' and being more than half
asleep I foolishly allowed him to put it to my nose.
In an instant the world swam round me, and then
everything became dark. The last thing that I
remember was a malignant grin of ferocious
triumph that flashed across the face that bent over
me. . . . .

"When I opened my eyes I was alone, my
turban and cummerbund were lying loose at my
feet; my pockets had been turned out, the contents
of my haversack littered the ground, and my heart
sank into a death-like faintness as I realized that
the little leather bag containing the Koh-i-noor
had been removed from my neck!!

"The tremendous fact stared me in the face.

The priceless gem, for which a king might have risked his empire, was gone! I started to my feet, vowing to recover the Koh-i-noor although I had to cut my way into the most secret recesses of the black pagoda. But which way was I to go? Seeking the high road I mechanically turned to the south, and I at once felt that my instinct had guided me aright. Keeping on the grassy side of the road I ran in silence, and in those days I could run like a Red Indian. After going at top speed for half a mile my heart gave a great bound as I saw a little ahead of me a short, dark figure. It was moving at a good pace, and I had still to gallop to win, but every now and then the figure would stop in order to hold something up to the light of the moon that had now just risen, and as it examined the thing the creature would hug itself in ecstasy, and leap high in the air with frantic joy.

"Where a break in the trees allowed the moonlight to stream in a bright cascade across the road the imp stopped once again in order to gloat upon the treasure. In another moment I had him tight by the throat, stretched on the ground beneath me. No sooner did he feel himself in my grasp than he became absolutely passive; he uttered no cry; he attempted no resistance,

and made no effort to escape, but accompanied
me back to my bivouac, dumb and torpid as a
dying fish.   Arrived at the fire, I saw, what
I had not discovered at his first appearance,
that the creature, so far from being an Eurasian
boy, was a middle-aged Purbeah dwarf, sufficiently light in colour to pass, when dressed
in European clothes, for an East Indian.   As
he paid no heed to my imperative demand for
the restitution of the diamond I produced a pistol
which, in the hurry of the pursuit, I had left in
my holster.   He regarded me stolidly, but made
no reply; in vain I thundered at him; in vain I
threatened his instant destruction; not a sign of
intelligence would he give; not a word would he
vouchsafe.   I examined his pockets, his clothes,
even his long hair, but the diamond was not to be
found.   Could he have flung it away on the high
road ?   The very thought so maddened me that I
seized him in my arms, and swung him over the
fire which was now burning briskly.   'Speak, you
stunted Satan,' I shouted, 'speak, or in you go!'
As I held him over the flames a tongue of fire shot
up, and singed one of his crooked legs.   The
pigmy's obstinacy was not proof against this
ordeal; he struggled fiercely, but I held him
tight.   Again the flame shot up, this time

wringing from him a smothered cry. As he opened his mouth I saw behind the blackened teeth a tell-tale radiance. In another moment the glorious gem was in my hand, and the dwarf, his motions stimulated by a well-planted kick, was speeding over the adjoining fields.

"After the overpowering excitement of such an adventure, sleep was impossible. I felt that the only way to obtain relief for my over-wrought nerves was a gallop through the cool night-air ; so, after once more carefully secreting the Koh-i-noor, I mounted my ever-ready horse, and betook myself to the road. It was lucky that I did so, for the dwarf, as I read afterwards when the Thuggi Commissioners published their famous report, made a bee-line from the toe of my boot to the Bêl, and, having roused his comrades by the announcement that the bearer of the Koh-i-noor was within two hundred yards of their nooses, he quickly assembled an armed party, which he led to my bivouac. They, however, found nothing there but the embers of the fire that had rendered me such signal assistance.

"I rode thirty miles that night before I drew rein, and although, when I dismounted, I believed myself to be in comparative safety, I, in point of fact, had halted at the most dangerous part of a

H

road known among the Thugs of the vicinity by
the humorous name of ' Strangle Street.' Nothing
unusual occurred, though, until I was well on my
next day's march, when, as I was passing a little
wood that bordered the highway, a bullet whistled
by my left ear, and the shot was followed by
another that displaced my turban. I had not
time to get at my pistols, and barely managed to
draw my sword when a man, well armed and
mounted, came charging down on me from the
cover of the trees. As he approached, I made my
horse swerve, and my assailant missed his swoop,
but he quickly wheeled, and made for me sword
in hand. He laid about him like a windmill, but
I carefully parried every cut. This must be the
Thug of war himself, I thought, and I shall have
to do all I know to beat him. At last I got a
chance. Warding off a tremendous back-hander
at my neck I gave him point at the fifth rib, and
he at once fell to the ground. At that moment
I heard the sound of cavalry coming down the
road at a gallop, it turned out to be a detachment
of mounted police, led by a Rissaldar.

" ' *Shahbash!* ' cried the leader. ' You have killed
the most famous robber of the country side ; we
heard that he had taken the road, and we have
been after him ever since the morning. You will

obtain a great name for this, but your presence at the Police-station is necessary in order that your deposition may be recorded.' And having given orders for the removal of the body, the Rissaldar, with me at his side, led his men across country to the place where the police were quartered.

" At the entrance to the village we were met by a party of elders headed by the Lumbardar, a fine old man of very dignified appearance. He gave me 'a kind and courteous greeting, praised my skill and daring, and thanked me in the name of the community for having freed the neighbourhood from an intolerable scourge. My conversation with the village worthies, followed by the tedious formalities attending the writing of my deposition, and the filling up of innumerable forms, rendered it late before I found myself at liberty. The Lum-. bardar then earnestly represented that as the comrades of the dead man would certainly lie in ambush! on the road, and would most probably kill me, to the enduring disgrace of the neighbourhood in general, and of that hamlet in particular, the most prudent course for me would be to remain in the village till daybreak, and then to accept the escort of the mounted police for about five miles, when I should be clear of 'Strangle

Street,' and should find myself in open country, where there was no danger of an ambuscade. I agreed to the proposal, and was invited to take up my quarters for the night in the police-station. I sat up till a late hour talking with the Rissaldar and his troopers, and listening to thrilling narratives of their encounters with Thugs and banditti. They thoughtfully provided me with a hookah, a form of smoking that I greatly disliked. I pretended, however, out of civility to my hosts, to take an occasional whiff at it, though in point of fact I inhaled none of the fumes. At last, one by one my interlocutors dropped off to sleep, and the Rissaldar, concluding a shocking picture of the lawlessness of the neighbourhood by the pious aspiration that the gods would some day come down and adjust matters themselves, spread his mat and composed himself to rest. I tried to follow suit, but for some inscrutable reason I could not sleep. I was weary enough, and was surrounded by the faithful guardians of the law, yet some internal monitor cautioned me to be on the alert, and I had every cause to be thankful that I heeded the warning.

"At midnight one of the party got up and, moving furtively, whispered something to the Rissaldar. I was at once all eyes and ears. 'He sleeps heavily,' said the first man, 'he is well hookah-stricken.'

"'He is certainly under the influence of the hookah,' replied the Rissaldar, 'but do you forget what the Guru said?'

"'Why wait for auspicious hours when the antelope is already in the net?' growled the other.

"'Respect is due to the Guru,' replied the Rissaldar, sternly, 'and I will not have the man killed till seven o'clock to-morrow morning. When he is eating his breakfast I will give the *shirnee* (signal), and you yourself shall throw the noose. Now go to sleep and do not provoke the anger of the goddess by disobeying the orders of the Guru.'

"Thus adjured, the first speaker, with a muttered protest, retired-to his mat, and the silence of the thannah was again unbroken save by the stertorous breathing of the sleepers.

"It was abundantly clear to me that this peaceful hamlet was, so far as I was concerned, decidedly unhealthy, so I waited for half an hour to make sure that everybody was asleep, and then departed without beat of drum. Before going, though, I drew the Rissaldar's sword, and placed the blade lightly across his throat, thus delicately hinting the penalty due to a man who would shed the blood of a guest. I might have spared myself the

trouble of this appeal to his sense of the obli-
gations of hospitality, for I learnt in Calcutta that
in the whole of Thugdom this village for cold-
blooded atrocity took the cake, and that the entire
community was composed of Thugs.   Police,
Rissaldar, Elders, Lumbardar, Ryots, and Guru ;
all were Thugs, deeply dyed in villainies innumerable, and flourishing on the proceeds of murder.
I stepped quietly out of the thannah, but, to
my extreme perplexity, could not find my horse.
It was, however, necessary to be off without
a moment's delay, so I prepared to continue
my journey on foot.   When I was clear of the
village I saw an animal grazing on a patch of
grass-land, and I recognized with intense delight
my faithful steed, which had strayed away in
search of food.   He was still saddled and bridled,
and in half no time I was on his back, making very
good time down the Grand Trunk."

The Colonel here lighted his sixth cheroot, and
called for another whiskey-peg.   "Now, if I were
to tell you fellows," he resumed, "all that happened to me during the remainder of my journey I
should keep you here till gun-fire, and we have
parade to-morrow, remember.   That Adjutant of
ours," and he shook his head in good-humoured
reprobation at me, "won't let us off, you know.

Terrible hot soldier, our Adjutant! so I must cut
my yarn short. Well, my life was attempted
in every conceivable fashion. Patriarchal old
gentlemen sitting under shady trees pressed me to
take shelter from the noon-day sun; honest
travellers entered unaffectedly into conversation
with me, offered me the most beautiful sweetmeats, and in frank good-fellowship begged me
to take a whiff of their hookahs; beautiful young
damsels, in the direst distress, implored my
assistance; wounded men rolled in agony on the
road, and besought me, in the name of Vishnu, to
give them a drink of water. But by this time I
was proof against the whole box and dice of them.
I was several times attacked by armed men, and
was twice wounded, once by a bullet, and once by
a spear, but I carried the Koh-i-noor in safety
through it all, and exactly three months after I
parted from John Lawrence at Lahore I entered
Calcutta, just hanging on by the slack, it is true,
for I was weary beyond words, and was, moreover,
badly hurt, and more than half-starved. I was
also consumed by fever, but I was *successful*, and,
I need not say, in consequence supremely happy.
It was Saturday night when I reached the capital.
On Sunday the Mint was closed, and by Monday
morning I was prostrated with ague. So I wrote

to Colonel A——, who was in charge of the Mint, asking him to come to my quarters, and receive the treasure.

"Within an hour of the despatch of my note I received a bit of paper on which was scrawled the words 'Babu Bhugwan Dass, Manager of the Calcutta Mint.' Having told my servant to show the gentleman in, a most respectable-looking individual entered my bedroom and told me that Colonel A—— had deputed him to receive the Koh-i-noor. I, however, flatly refused to give up the diamond to any one but the Colonel himself, and my visitor seemed much hurt at my want of faith. Finding me obdurate, he begged that I would at any rate favour him with a glimpse of the famous gem. But here again I was recalcitrant. In his eagerness to prove how baseless were my suspicions, he advanced, chattering volubly the while, to the side of my bed, and as he drew near, I saw lying in his sleeve a yellow silk handkerchief, one end of which he held in his hand, 'all in the old sweet way.' The sight of this bit of silk was enough for me—he would not be warned off, so I pulled out a pistol, and blazed. The bullet struck him in the hip, and, with a yell of pain, he fell sprawling on the matting.

"At that moment Colonel A—— arrived, accom-

panied by two European assistants. I knew the
Colonel well, there was no doubt about *him.*

" 'Sorry to have spoilt your Manager, Colonel,'
I said, ' but the beggar was going to noose me.'

" ' My Manager ! ' exclaimed the Colonel, ' Mr.
Purvis here is my Manager,' and he indicated one
of the attendant Europeans. ' This fellow,' continued he, looking at the wounded man, .'is a
perfect stranger.'

" ' He is not a stranger to me though,' said
I, regarding the self-styled Babu more closely.
' Why, Colonel, as I am a living sinner, he is one
of the men that tried to enter my service as syce
just before I left Lahore ! '

" There was no doubt about it ; the rascal was
the least respectable of the three disguised Thugs,
and was afterwards recognized by the Police as
one Feringeah, a well-known desperado who had
poisoned my syce, and was ' wanted ' also for
murder in the Dooab, where he was shortly afterwards tried and hanged."

" Did you get any reward for all this, Colonel ? "
inquired the Doctor.

" Reward, Doctor, bless you, no ! I did, some
years afterwards, suggest to the India Office and
the Horse Guards that such peculiarly good work
as mine merited some slight Government recog-

nition—C.B., good service pension, unattached majority, or any trifle that might be going. But you know the style. I was met by the reply— 'Nothing on record.' As if that was *my* fault. —My prophetic soul! it's twelve o'clock. There goes the Adjutant. We shall all be late for parade to-morrow. Good-night t'ye!"

NANGLE'S NIECE.

"Perhaps the occasion when I found myself, in more senses than one, most thoroughly up a tree," remarked Colonel Bowlong, "was when I brought Nangle's niece out of the fort of Comusgunge. Nanny Nangle was three years old, her parents had perished in the massacre at Cuttlepore, and we all said that the miracle by which the child had escaped would be more than equalled if her uncle succeeded in rearing her. Major Nangle, I must tell you, while he was the soul of good-nature, was the very incarnation of laziness. How his work was performed no man could tell; as for his private establishment it was the veritable home of the sluggard ; and had the care of stable and kennel depended upon the proprietor, his horses and dogs would have starved. He, however, possessed a butler, old Ram Bux, the prince of extortioners, but a first-rate domestic administrator, who always

turned out Nangle and his animals in unexceptionable form.

"When Nanny arrived in a clothes-basket with
one or two of the survivors from Cuttlepore, the
old butler admitted her to a share of his super-
vision with the solicitude that he would have
extended to a supernumerary puppy or an addi-
tional pony; I need not tell you that every mouth
he had to cater for helped to swell the old sinner's
nefarious income; and Nanny's broth and pudding
were furnished with the regularity of the stable
gram and the dog-biscuits; in fact, her maintenance soon formed the most profitable item in Ram
Bux's weekly budget, where it figured under the
somewhat vague heading of 'chile expennis.'

"Nanny was a fair-haired, chubby little creature,
with large round eyes, and a wide mouth always
on the smile. She was full of fun, and her tongue
was never still. I seldom rode past Nangle's
house without first looking in to have a talk with
the child and to give her some sugar-plums, called
in her language 'tchweeties.' A week or two after
Nanny's arrival it became apparent to us all that
she had hopped out of the frying-pan into the
fire. Our garrison consisted of three sepoy foot-
regiments and two squadrons of the now notorious
Numuckhirami Lancers, a detachment of which

had started the revolt at Cuttlepore, and it was soon pretty plain that these squadrons were about to play the same game here.

"Late one Saturday evening news reached the General that, on the following morning, we were all to be scuppered in church. Upon this the old chief immediately summoned the entire European community to his house in order to decide upon a course of action. As the last man entered the Brigadier's compound the eight o'clock gun fired, and then, as though it had been a preconcerted signal, there arose a most violent clamour in the lines, shouting, drumming, bugling, firing, as though Hades had broken loose.

"'My informant has misled me,' said the General, calmly, 'I was told that the rising was fixed for to-morrow; there is no time to be lost. The ladies and children will start at once for Allahabad. The officers will accompany me to the lines.'

"There was no time for discussion, horses and vehicles were on the spot, and in less than ten minutes a dozen carriages were rattling along the Allahabad road, while the General, accompanied by some five-and-twenty officers, rode in the direction of the tumult. As we cantered across the Parade-ground we encountered a squadron of native Lancers uttering wild shouts of 'Deen!' and

making for the European quarter. Placing himself at our head, the brave old General drew his
sword and ordered us to charge. At 'em we went,
full tilt; they were coming on at the gallop, and
we met fair; their lances were slung and we took
'em by surprise. The shock was tremendous; in
half a second men and horses were rolling about in
the moonlight like scattered nine-pins. I cut
down three of the mutineers and was then knocked
silly with the butt end of a lance. When I
recovered my senses I was lying in a buggy,
spinning along with the ladies towards Allahabad.
I then learnt what had happened. We cut up
the leading cavalry in style, but it cost us half
our strength, and while we were in disorder down
came the second squadron and sent us to the
right-about; the General was killed and there was
no one to give orders, so the survivors of our
party joined the main body of the fugitives. I
was picked up by Nangle and was carried across
his saddle till we caught up the carriages. We
were not pursued very far; and after hard going
all night, when the day broke we saw the walls
of Allahabad gleaming in the rising sun.

"As we drove through the gateway some one
sang out, 'Hullo!' Nangle, where's the little
girl?'

"'By Heaven!' gasped the Major, pale as death, 'I left her in the bungalow.'

"While still speaking he turned his horse's head, and if some one had not seized the bridle he would have galloped back to certain destruction ; indeed, for some hours afterwards physical compulsion was necessary to prevent his leaving the fort. I never saw a man so transformed as was the unhappy Major; his usual careless, sleepy manner had changed to an almost maniacal restlessness, and for a week or so it required all the watchfulness that we could exert to prevent his slipping out and returning to the station ; but as the days rolled by, he gradually sank into his old lethargy; and after a time the child, who at first had been the only subject of his thoughts, was hardly ever alluded to.

"As soon as I was well enough to get about I began to make inquiries concerning poor Nanny's fate, and from what I gathered from spies, and native fugitives I came to the conclusion that her life had for a second time been miraculously preserved. Information from various quarters focussed into the fact that a little European girl had been sold by an officer's kitmutgar to the Nawab of Comusgunge, a monster in whose hands the child's future would be too hideous to contemplate. Something assured me that the little captive was none other than our Nanny, and, impelled no less by gratitude to Nangle than by my affection for the child, I determined at any risk to rescue her without delay. Having acquainted the officer in command with my resolve, I received his permission to take whatever steps I thought necessary. Now Comusgunge was strongly fortified and well-manned, the surrounding country was swarming with mutineers, and but few men could be spared from the Allahabad garrison, so an attack by main force was out of the question. After a long consultation with Kamran, the chief scout, I formed my plan of action, and, one moonless night, shortly after sunset, he and I left Allahabad with a small party of Sikh cavalry. Taking the most direct road to Comusgunge we proceeded for about four hours at a good trot. Suddenly Kamran laid his hand upon my horse's neck, whispering that we were approaching the rebel stronghold and must now proceed cautiously. Leaving the beaten track we walked our horses warily over the grass for about half a mile, and then halted under the shadow of some trees, while Kamran should go forward to reconnoitre. Throwing his reins to one of the sowars the scout crept towards the fortress in our front, which

in the mist might have been mistaken for a large
grey rock.   In less than half an hour he returned,
and whispered that the great gate had just been
opened in order to admit a number of country
grain-carts, and if we were quick we might slip in
with the rear waggons, overpower the guard, and
carry off the child in the confusion.

"This was not exactly the plan that had been
decided upon, but it seemed under the circumstances as good as any other.   In another minute
we were in the saddle cantering over the turf towards the gate, the shouts of the bullock-drivers
and the groaning of the heavily-laden wheels
effectually drowning all sounds of our approach.
As the last cart rumbled through the archway I
cut down the sleepy sentry, and half a minute
afterwards my Sikhs had sabred the entire guard.
The whole thing was done so quickly and quietly
that not a shot was fired nor a word uttered.
As for the cart-drivers, when they saw what was
going on they threw themselves into the ditch
and, swimming across like water-rats, made for
the open country, leaving their convoy to its
fate.

"I now resolved to try to get hold of the child
without causing an alarm, which, as the fort was
crammed with men, might have resulted in the

I

slaughter of us all, for the sowars were not a dozen, all told. So, leaving the Sikhs in charge of the gate, with Kamran as my guide, I made for the women's apartments in the interior of the fort. Not a soul was stirring, but from many quarters there came a great sound of music and revelry, which Kamran explained by the word *Ramzan.* The Nawab's retainers were celebrating the termination of the Muslim Lent; and our progress was unchallenged. When we reached the Zenana gate we saw a huge Abyssinian negro, armed with a short curved sword and a brazen shield, leaning in a half-doze against the door-post. In the twinkling of an eye Kamran's long dagger, driven violently down where the neck and shoulders join, had turned the African's doze into the sleep that knows no waking. The victim fell with a groaning sigh, and lay motionless.

"Paying no further attention to him, we entered the hall as cautiously as cats on ice, and, stepping over the sleeping forms of three or four slave-women, we ascended a narrow stone staircase, lighted at intervals by dim oil lamps. Kamran appeared to be perfectly familiar with the place, following all its windings and turnings with the ease of a denizen—in point of fact there were few fortresses in Oudh that this able scout did

not know as thoroughly as he knew his own little
hut on the Goomtee. We soon found ourselves
in a long passage, at the end of which hung a
heavy felt purdah, and, silently lifting this, we
entered a large sleeping-chamber. Scattered
around on mats and cushions were nine or ten
sleeping women of various ages, and on a small
rug in the middle of them, like a wee white lamb
in a wolf's den, lay my little pal Nanny. She
was wide awake, staring at a moth in the lamp,
and crooning scraps of a nursery song. The child
recognized me at once, and holding out her
chubby little hand, cried, with her old cheerful
smile, 'You brought me tchweetie, Bowlong?
Long time I get no tchweetie.'

"Whispering to her not to speak, I lifted
her in my arms, but as I was turning to go I
most unfortunately trod on the finger of an old
woman who was sleeping near. The beldame,
uttering an exclamation of pain, sat up and
rubbed her eyes. I remained perfectly still,
hoping that she would go to sleep again without
discovering me, but Nanny, always full of conversation, remarked audibly,

"'Dat ole woman 'mack me last night, tread
finger again.'

Hearing Nanny's voice the hag rose to her feet

and, realizing that some one was carrying off her prisoner, she began to scream blue murder. In half a second all the women were awake, and seeing two strange men in the sacred precincts of the harem, they began to raise an outcry that might have been heard at Allahabad. Such a scare you never witnessed. It was a regular harem-scarum—ha! ha!

"'Fly for your life!' shouted Kamran, and, pitching the scurrying women to right and left, he made a plunge for the door and led the way down the corridor. With difficulty shaking off two clamouring harridans who had seized me by the legs I hastily followed the scout, but in the darkness, losing sight of my guide, I took a wrong turn. The building was a perfect rabbit-warren of passages, and when at last I found myself in the open air, I discovered to my extreme bewilderment that instead of emerging upon the large courtyard I had entered an enclosed garden. It was impossible to retrace my steps, for the building that I had just quitted began to ring with a babel of voices in every corner and to sparkle with lights at every casement. To increase the anxiety of the situation a big drum began to sound angrily from the central turret, while shouts and musket-shots from the direction of the gate told me that my followers were fighting for their lives. A large door leading from the house into the garden was now thrown open, and twenty or thirty armed men, some of them carrying lanterns, began to search for intruders among the bushes. I was standing near a large peepul-tree in the centre of the garden, and, seeing that it afforded our only chance of safety, I climbed with my little charge among the branches. After carefully searching every square foot of the garden the men assembled under the tree where we were roosting.

"'Old Khanum was wrong,' said one; 'the Feringhee never entered the garden.'

"'If he crossed the court,' said another, 'he has by this time gone to *Jehannum.*'

"'Lucky for him if he has,' said a third, 'for the Khan has sworn to skin him alive for slaying the Hubshi.'

"'Bowlong dear, where my tchweetie?' suddenly asked Nanny in a stage-whisper.

"I luckily recollected that I had in my pocket a piece of sugar-cane that I had brought to reward my horse with after his long trot. This I handed to my young companion, who chewed it appreciatively. Some one in authority now entered the garden; he was accompanied by a number of men

carrying matchlocks and torches.   I suppose it was
the Khan.

"'Enough for to-night,' he said, 'the gates are
closed, the sentries doubled, the sons of swine that
killed the guard have been sent to Iblis, not one
has left the fort, and in the morning we shall
certainly discover the Feringhee and the baba.
Inshallah !   What's that ?' he ejaculated, as
Nanny's piece of sugar-cane fell upon his head.

"'Only old Khanum's monkey, Huzoor!' replied
one of the men, jerking a stone into the tree;
'the animal lives in this garden.'

"After a few more remarks, the entire party
moved in the direction of the house.   In a minute
or two the great door was closed and bolted, and
the garden was again dark and silent.   I then
removed my restraining hand from poor Nanny's
mouth, and was overwhelmed with the little
damsel's reproaches for not allowing her to call to
one of the men, whom she had recognized, to
hand up her 'thugar-thtick.'

"Here a nice quandary!   I was already
beginning to feel cramped, and I certainly could
not remain in the tree holding the child for a
lengthened spell.   Without the shadow of a doubt
soon after the sun rose I should be made a prisoner.
I could not escape through the house, for the little

postern by which I had emerged was now closed, and the garden was surrounded with high walls.

"While I was taking in all the beauties of the situation, something passed beneath the tree—it was a jackal, then came another, followed by a third. The thought at once occurred to me that where these jacks got in I could get out, so descending from my perch, with the child in my arms, I followed the animals on tip-toe, and perceived that, after making the circuit of the garden, they vanished behind a large bush at the end of the central walk. This bush, I found, concealed a hole in the wall through which ran a small water-course leading from the garden fountains; the passage was just large enough to allow me to get through with a squeeze, but it was too small for me to pass it with the child. I tried to persuade the little creature to creep through in front of me, but shaking her head violently she said the passage was 'black bogey-hole,' and resolutely refused to make the attempt. In order to encourage her I crawled through to the other side, and to my surprise found myself outside the fort walls on the margin of the moat. When Nanny saw my head reappearing she clapped her hands and cried 'Peep bo, froggie!' but nothing would induce her either to precede or to follow me through the culvert. This was very mortifying, but what was to be done? It was impossible to go without Nanny, so I sorrowfully led her back to the peepul-tree, and, sitting down with my back against the trunk and the child sleeping in my arms, I waited philosophically for the morning—and its developments.

"I have observed that in even the most critical affairs of life circumstances present themselves by means of which a sharp fellow can extricate himself from the very tightest toils. It requires *nous*, of course, and the application of the principle is limited to a select few—most men never recognize the opportunity. Dangerous, therefore, as my position was, I was convinced that a chance of escape would sooner or later present itself. When day dawned I thought it prudent to re-ascend the tree, and Nanny, who for the last hour had been prattling like a young mina, wanted to know the reason.

"'Why you climb tree like monkey?' she inquired.

"'Because,' I answered, 'if those Moormen catch me I shall be skinned alive.'

"On hearing this Nanny disclosed much intelligent interest.

"'Will they 'kin you with a pin?'

"'No, my dear, with a sharp knife.'

" ' Blood come ? '

" ' Yes, plenty of blood.'

" ' You cry ? ' she inquired, with plaintive sympathy.

" ' Very loud.'

" Nanny's eyes opened wide.

" ' May Nanny see, Bowlong dear ? '

" ' Not if Nanny talks so loud,' I said severely; ' little girls that talk loud never see people skinned.'

" This had the effect of somewhat checking the flow of my companion's speech, and in the silence that ensued I had an opportunity of carefully observing my surroundings. To scale the walls was impossible, for they were enormously high, and there were no trees near them ; but I noticed, what had escaped me in the darkness, that in the wall to my left front was a door that clearly gave access to the courtyard. This, however, brought me but cold comfort, seeing that the door was fastened by a padlock, and even if it had been open it presented no advantage, for to show myself in the courtyard by daylight was simply to invite immediate death or capture.

" ' Dere's old Khanum,' said Nanny, ' de ole woman dat always 'mack me. She come to feed Bandhur.'

" Turning my head, I saw an old woman, carrying an earthen pot, enter the garden from the
postern-door, and in response to her call a huge
ape came bounding towards her from a distant
hiding-place. After the animal had devoured its
breakfast, the old woman played with it, holding
up her bunch of keys for the animal to jump
at. The ape made several springs and at last
clutched the keys, which he put into his mouth.
In vain his mistress tried to recover the booty;
the creature, after hopping round her mowing and
grinning for a minute or two, made a bee-line for
his lair, passing in his course under our tree. At
the foot of the tree lay the piece of sugar-cane that
Nanny, the night before, had let fall among the
Khan's retainers; the monkey at once dropped the
keys and, seizing the delicacy, pursued his way
without stopping, while the old woman, unaware of
what had happened, followed him, hurling clods and
stones and asthmatic execrations. When she had
gone by I slid down the trunk, and, having picked
up the keys, rejoined Nanny in the tree, where I
proceeded to examine my prize. Upon the bunch
there were only two door-keys, one of medium
size, evidently belonging to the postern, and a
larger one that I felt sure opened the door leading
into the court.

" While Khanum was pursuing the monkey, the morning-gun was fired (their hours were latish at Comusgunge), and the report was followed by the tap of a tom-tom and the sound of a horn. Soon the hum that marks the awakening life of a large native fortress began to make itself heard, and I realized that the crisis was approaching. Presently a key turned in the lock of the great door, which, creaking on its hinges, admitted a crowd of men, who had come to renew the search of the preceding night. To my infinite concern I observed that they did not now confine their scrutiny to the shrubs and undergrowth, but sent one of their number to explore the branches of every tree large enough to shelter a man. They worked slowly and systematically, and it seemed as though nothing short of supernatural power could save me now. Yet I did not even then despair. It was clear that my chance had not come yet, for I attached no importance to the episode of the drain, seeing that the child's resistance had nullified that apparent opportunity, and I felt satisfied that the situation, like all the many other positions of danger that I have occupied, would carry with it the materials of escape.

" ' Those men looking for Bandhur ? ' inquired Nanny.

" ' No, dear, not for Bandhur,' I replied.

" ' Then they come to 'kin you, I tink,' she rejoined, with animation.

" ' Hush, hush ! ' I whispered, as the searchers were coming unpleasantly close, ' if you hold your tongue, Nanny, I will take you outside and give you sugar-cane and prunes, and oh ! *such* a lot of luddoos.' This appeal to her better feelings, lulled the vivacious little maid into temporary silence, and before she spoke again I was prepared to carry the first part of my promise into effect, for the chance had come."

The Colonel paused in order to light a fresh cheroot, and as he slowly puffed it into a glow he looked round the circle of his listeners with an amused smile at our expectant faces.

" How in the world did you do it, Colonel ? " we asked in chorus.

" How did I do it ? Why in the most simple and natural manner possible. As the search-party drew near my hiding-place, I noticed that the sun, which was well up, was rapidly losing its lustre, its beams were growing murky, and a dark rim was stealing over its disc. I did not require a second look to tell me that what I saw was the penumbra of an eclipse, and I re-collected that this was the day on which the almanack had foretold a total obscuration of the sun. As the light rapidly faded, the men below began to look anxiously to the East; they advanced more and more hesitatingly, and the zeal of the hunt visibly slackened. When the gloom deepened, they gathered into a knot and took hurried counsel together, the result being a laughing stampede back to the house. Luckily for us, these warriors did not quite like being caught in the uncanny darkness caused by the sun's struggle with the dragon.

" ' I tink all people go to bye-o,' whispered Nanny, somewhat puzzled. ' I want my conjee, Bowlong dear? I, too, velly sleepy,' and she yawned and stretched herself.

" I had precious little time to talk to Nanny now. No sooner was the garden clear than I descended with her to the ground, nipped like lightning to the courtyard-door, found to my immense delight that the key fitted, and then stepping gingerly across the quadrangle, passed the gate guard and sentry unobserved in the obscurity, and before you could say ' knife ' I was making the best time I could up the high-road.

" ' Now give prunes and luddoos,' commanded Nanny, in the tone of one not to be trifled with any longer. 'Bowlong, you promised you give *such* a lot of tchweeties.'

"I assured her that in an hour or two she should roll in sweeties, and then, as I had to make hay before the sun shone, I kept my breath for my running, and continued to carry my little prize at the double towards Allahabad. As the eclipse disappeared I, still going strong, ran up against a horseman, whom, in the returning light, I recognized as the faithful Kamran.

"'Welcome, Sahib!' he cried, triumphantly. 'I knew you would free yourself, and I have been waiting here for you these six hours with your horse. The Sikhs, alas! have all been cut up. We are certain to be pursued. Mount, Sahib, and ride hard.'

"As the mid-day gun fired from the ramparts of Allahabad we cheerily answered the challenge of the sentry and cantered over the drawbridge. Nanny, though a trifle hungry and excited with her ride, was none the worse for the adventure, and when her uncle's violent and somewhat hysterical greetings intermitted sufficiently to allow her to speak, she gave the assembled garrison an animated and somewhat jocose account of the episodes of the night. She concluded by remarking with a decidedly injured air, 'Naughty

Bandhur took my thugar-thtick, Nanny got no tchweeties, and they never 'kinned Bowlong.'"

"What became of Miss Nangle, Colonel?" asked Snapper, when the laugh over the child's innocent truculence had subsided.

"Nanny, if you please, is now Her Grace the Duchess of Falconbridge and Mistress of the Fans to the Queen," replied the Colonel.

"Did you ever remind her of this little adventure, sir?"

"Not I, Her Grace and I move in different planes; you may take your oath she knows nothing whatever about the affair. What could a child of that age remember? and she would never hear the story from Nangle, it showed up his own carelessness, don't you see. Would you believe it, when I referred to the matter one night at the 'Senior,' only ten years after I put his rescued niece into his arms, old Nangle couldn't recollect a word of it? Why! the old idiot almost as good as said that the thing had never happened!" and the Colonel indignantly threw the end of his cheroot into a corner and called for his carriage.

COLONEL BOWLONG AND THE SEVEN SISTERS.

——o——

"WHAT was the greatest danger that you ever encountered, Colonel?" The querist, as usual, was Snapper, who was always hunting the good-natured chief for a tale. Colonel Bowlong had just risen from a game of whist, at which fortune had steadily followed him round the table, and as he lighted a six-inch cheroot we knew by the radiance of his face that he was good for a yarn.

"My greatest danger, Snap!"—puff-puff-puff—"well, indeed, that's hard to say, that's precious hard to say. I was in a pretty tight corner at Comusgunge, and I don't think my life would have commanded a favourable rate of insurance when I missed my ship in the Bay of Bengal, but I am inclined to think that I passed through my greatest peril at Saugur, in the summer of 185—. We marched from Jubbulpore in January of that year, and the night before we reached Saugur the Colonel, having called up all the

Subalterns to his tent, addressed us something as
follows :—

" 'Look here, you boys, for the last ten years
the Pans haven't had a married man among
'em, except Vickers,'—Vickers was the vet—'and
you know what *his* folly cost us. Since that man
haltered himself our annual loss in horses has
pretty nearly equalled the casualties of the whole
Sutlej campaign ! I can trust the Captains ; I can
trust the Majors ; and, begad, I can trust myself ;
but—I am afraid for you soft Subs. Now, by the
King of Clubs, if any of you lads brings a woman
into the Regiment, I'll—I'll——' The Colonel's
anger at the very idea so overpowered him that he
could not finish the sentence, and he abruptly
dismissed us with a wave and a snort.

" Our arrival at Saugur was the signal for all
sorts of gaieties : tiffins, dinners, picnics, dances,
and races were the order of the day, and we
youngsters very soon made the acquaintance of all
the girls in the place. They were a nice lot, and
in the main good, sensible young women who
assisted to make things pleasant for the community
without looking at every bachelor they came across
as a possible husband. There was one family,
however, the Puckerows, that I observed all the
men fought desperate shy of. The father, a

retired officer, was dead, and the mother, with seven unmarried daughters, occupied a large rambling house in a tangled compound just out of cantonments. This house was popularly called the 'Spider's Web,' the occupants,—two bullock-bandy loads of 'em, by Jove!—used to come to everything in the station that was going as regularly as a parson attends church. Each of the Puckerows had a nickname : the mother was called the 'Spider,' the girls were the 'Oonth,'* the 'Pouchie,'† the 'Flycatcher,' 'Pickles,' 'Fluffy,' 'Ginger,' and 'Jo.' Colonel Harde regarded this truly formidable family with the liveliest apprehension, and frequent and solemn were his warnings to us regarding them. He pointed out how they had been for many years upon the war-path, and knew every artifice of the old campaigner so thoroughly that if a fellow spoke to one of them but three times in one week, material would be afforded whereby the old spider would mesh him into an engagement.'

" 'They have tried every arm of the service without success, and if they catch a Pandour,' added he, with pathetic fury, ' the Regiment deserves to be disbanded ! '

---

* Camel.   † Insect.

"We all assured the Colonel that nothing was further from our minds than wedding-cake, and that if it were otherwise we would not go to the Puckerow nest for a helpmate, even though there were not another girl in Asia. But the old warrior only shook his head despondingly, and muttered something about the proverbial weakness of subalterns and the guile of the garrison girl.

"Time went on, and when the ground was a bit soft after the summer rains we had a sky-meeting, and I rode my mare *Chitmunk* in the Garrison Hurdles. It was a stiffish course; a lot of men were spilt; and, to my surprise, I won the cup by a length. I was in great spirits at this my first score between the flags, and at the race-ball that night I drank half a drop more fizz than was quite good for me. You may imagine that I had trifled a bit with the wine-cup when I tell you that I found myself waltzing with one of the Puckerow girls. Each time that I passed the Colonel his face grew redder, and his warning frown more ominous; once I distinctly heard him stamp his foot, and, well—it—was *not* a blessing that he murmured. But I was in no humour to comply with the storm signals. After the dance, my partner asked me to take her into the supper-room. There was a small table by the window that afforded a secluded retreat, and Miss Puckerow thought she would sit there. I don't know what I said, I only know that after talking very volubly for a few minutes I suddenly woke to the consciousness that my companion was looking at me tenderly, and was saying something with horrifying earnestness. I listened with a palpitating heart, and my hair bristled with terror as I heard her say,—

"'And therefore, Mr. Bowlong, as I have heard the truth from your own lips, I will gladly be your loving little wife.'

"I had been hooked by the 'Pouchie'!

"Freed from my passing lunacy, and shivering with the shock as I realized the full meaning of my recent action, I hurried into the garden. I don't know what led me there, perhaps it was the instinctive desire of a hunted animal to get away from its pursuer. As I left the well-lighted verandah I ran violently against a man emerging from the darkness. It was Charlie Rochester, who had been seeing a lady into her carriage.

"'Hullo! Bowlong!' cried he, 'you seem in a precious hurry. What's up?'

"I took him by the arm, and led him into a side-walk. 'I'm ruined, Rochester, smashed up, pounded and ruined,' I gasped.

"'What's the figure?' he inquired, adding kindly, 'I landed a hundred gold mohurs on the *Chitmunk* to-day, you can have 'em if they'll do you any good.'

"'No, no, it's not mohurs—it's matrimony!' I groaned.

"'That's a sight worse than any amount of debt,' said he, gravely; 'but let's hear all about it. I've been cornered myself, Dukie, before now. Who is she?'

"'The "Pouchie,"'" I whispered faintly. Rochester gave a low whistle.

"'Thunder and turf! she'll land you if any one can.' He mused for a moment, 'Hold on a bit,' he cried, 'I've got it. Go in and propose to the balance.'

"'The balance,' I stammered, 'what the deuce do you mean?'

"'I mean this,' he said; 'propose to all of them, one after the other, and seven to one you'll escape in the confusion.'

"'It's eight to one, Charlie, there's the "Spider" to reckon with.'

"'Blow the "Spider," propose to her too. There goes the 'Roast Beef,' and I have to take Mrs. Honeysuckle into supper,' and he left me to consider his advice.

"On examining the programme I found that there were just six more waltzes. Having diligently searched out the 'Pouchie's' sisters, I engaged one of them for each dance, and deliberately proposed to each of my partners as we spun round. I need not say that I was accepted by them *all*. Desperation had now so completely got the better of me that I think if there had been an 'extra' I should have tried my luck with the 'Spider' also.

"I dutifully assisted my seven brides-elect into the two family bullock-coaches, and was over-whelmed by a honeyed chorus of 'Good-night, *good*-night, Mr. Bowlong,' accompanied by an amorous flutter of small lace handkerchiefs from seven different windows. I told myself that I deserved kicking. I never felt so small, so utterly mean, in my life. But I had to pull myself together to meet the tempest that would burst in fury upon me in the morning, for it was certain that as soon as they reached home each dear girl would confide her little secret to mamma, and a compari-son of notes would convert that aviary of doves into an eyry of eagles. I knew that family pretty well by repute, and rumour had it that each member was appallingly endowed with the gift of speech.

"Next morning seven triangular pink notes were

brought in with my early tea. I had not the courage to read them, and to this day I don't know what they contained. Shortly afterwards I received a square, formidable-looking document, in the uncompromising up-and-down hand of Mrs. Puckerow; it was superscribed 'urgent.' I would gladly have chucked this missive on one side with the others, but there was a certain imperative, dominating air about it that compelled respect, and I opened it after the manner of a man under the influence of hypnotism. It was curt, and, to my guilty conscience, lucidly menacing. Mrs. Puckerow desired me to call and see her at my '*very earliest convenience* on business of *extreme importance.*' All these letters had evidently been written the night before, for they arrived at gun-fire, and the ladies could hardly have been at their desks before daylight. I sent Mrs. Puckerow's letter over to Rochester, asking for advice how to act. He sent it back with a pencil scrawl, 'Say you were screwed.' This was not far from the truth. I still felt a bit chippy after the race committee's champagne, so I had the mare out for an hour's ride in the cool morning air, and then feeling that I was as fit for the ordeal as I ever should be, I put my horse's head in the direction of the Web.

" As I turned into the large neglected compound

I met ' Jo ' Puckerow in her old blue habit going
out for a rather late morning ride. She shook
her whip at me, and said in mock indignation :
' You're a nice young man to go and offer marriage to seven innocent maidens in one night, as
if you were the Sultan of Turkey, or the man in
the parable.' Jo's Biblical training, I am afraid,
was slightly defective. ' I'll tell you what it is, Mr.
Bowlong, you deserve to get it hot and heavy, and
you will, too, before it's all over ; there's such a
row going on in that house at this moment that
I advise you to turn round and come for a canter
with me.'

" ' You're very good, but I *must* go and see your
mother and get it over,' I said, not quite knowing
what to make of Miss Jo's chaff, for she had as
much cause to be angry as any of them.

" ' Get it over ! ' she laughed, ' get it *over !*
You're pretty hopeful about it, I must say. You
propose to all of us in the evening, and then ride
over to morning-tea and say, " So sorry, quite a
mistake, meant entirely some other thing, la-di-
da," and expect to get it *over !* It's very clear you
don't know my sisters—or my mother.'

" ' Miss Puckerow,' I said, gathering a sudden
glimpse of hope from her laughing eyes, ' I can
see that you understand it all, and mean to be

my friend.' She hadn't said anything to warrant that, but it formed a good working hypothesis. 'I know you'll help me. Tell me, like a good girl, how to get out of this stupid business.'

"She thought a moment, and then replied,— 'Well, I'll tell you what you had better do. Of course you mean to say you were tipsy, don't you, now? And my belief is that you were a little bit that way ; but that won't serve with the girls ; Pouchie and Ginger' (Jo was the only one of them that recognised the family nicknames) 'have had a tremendous quarrel about you already. Pouchie says she accepted you *first*, and has the prior claim, and Ginger declares that as you proposed to her *last*, you clearly meant to throw over the others ; and I am sure mother will not listen to the excuse of too much wine for a moment, unless you explain that you were tipsy when you spoke to my sisters, but sober when you proposed to me. She'll then think it a very good joke, and will laugh at the others. Don't be afraid that I'm going to catch you. After the way you have behaved I wouldn't have you, no, not if you were to ask me a hundred times over. You're safe enough with me. When the excitement at home has settled down a little I will quietly throw you over. Will that do ?'

" 'You undertake to throw me over, Miss Puckerow?' I said, doubtfully.

" 'Most solemnly,' she said, holding out her hand.

" We shook hands on the compact, and she cantered down the drive, while I, with a sinking heart, walked my horse up to Mrs. Puckerow's door.

" I was but eighteen you must remember, and it was a bit of a trial to meet seven justly exasperated ladies, each of them considerably my senior in years, and immeasurably my superior in debating power. I was ushered into the big drawing-room, and left for a while to meditate amid the massive black-wood furniture. As I entered the room I was aware of a confused clamour of distant voices in highly emotional dialogue, and I confess that I trembled. Shortly after the servant had left me these lively sounds gave place to a gruesome silence, infinitely more ominous and awe-inspiring than the preceding notes of strife, for it told me that the combatants had now joined forces, and were advancing with concentrated power and unity of purpose upon a single objective point—and that point poor me ! The door opened with a majestic swing, and the six Miss Puckerows, headed by their mamma, entered the room in stately procession. Each lady glided to a seat in awful silence, like a shoal of sharks converging upon a swimmer. They looked at me, and their eyes flashed indignant reproaches, and as I modestly lowered my gaze, and played nervously with my riding-whip, I heard in the very rustle of their skirts an expression of wrath and scorn.

"After a preparatory cough Mrs. Puckerow spoke as follows :—' I believe, Mr. Bowlong, that I am addressing an officer and a gentleman ? ' I bowed. ' A Cornet of the King's Pandours ? ' Again I bowed. ' Then I desire you, sir, to explain your unprecedented conduct of last night towards my daughters —the daughters of the late Major Puckerow, retired, your superior officer. I need not undertake the painful recital of what occurred at the ball, all here present remember it but too well, but I demand, and I have a just and absolute right to demand, an explanation of your extra-ordinary behaviour.'

" ' I'm afraid, Mrs. Puckerow, I must plead guilty to an indiscretion,' I began.

" ' An indiscretion ! ' exclaimed Mrs. Puckerow, with a tragic -start. ' You call proposing to my girls one after the other as fast as you can speak the words only an *indiscretion !* ' and the speaker appeared to my bewildered gaze to swell venomously.

" ' I mean, madam,' I replied, ' and I say it with

shame, that last evening I drank more champagne than was good for me, and I have come to offer my sincere apologies to your daughters and to yourself.'

"'Too much champagne!' cried Mrs. Puckerow in threatening crescendo, 'then, sir, you must be tried by court-martial and cashiered, drummed out of your Regiment for conduct unbecoming an officer and a gentleman. But *that* is a matter for Colonel Harde and your superiors. All that I have to say to you is this, tell me at once, here, before them all, which of my poor dear girls it is that you desire to make your wife.' And she fixed me with such a stony stare, and the twelve grey eyes around me were so paralyzing, that although I longed to say, 'not one of them,' I could not get my vocal muscles to frame the words, so, acting in conformity with Jo's suggestion, I replied with affected frankness :—

"'To tell you the truth, Mrs. Puckerow, although I greatly admire all your charming daughters, my affections are set upon only one of them.'

"'And which is that?' inquired the Spider, with a slight thaw in her tone.

"I hesitated, could I, dare I, trust my fate to an inmate of the Web?

"'I may as well tell you at once,' continued

Mrs. Puckerow, 'that my daughter Mary' (that was Jo), 'when she heard how you had behaved to her sisters, at once renounced her claim upon you. She said that nothing on earth should induce her to marry a man who could be guilty of such extremely heartless conduct, so I hope it's not Mary.'

" This decided me.

" 'What crushing luck,' I murmured, with an air of the deepest grief; 'your daughter Mary *is* the one I love.'

Upon this the six young ladies rose, and without so much as bestowing a glance in my direction, swept like scornful swans from the room, leaving me alone with their mother.

" 'Well, well, cheer up, don't despair, my dear boy,' said the old lady, gaily, 'faint heart never won fair lady; no doubt Mary spoke hastily. I will be your advocate, and I may tell you that in matters of importance dear Mary always allows herself to be guided by me.'

" I rose, shuddering, and took my leave.

"Late that evening I received a note full of effusive congratulation from Mrs. Puckerow. She had spoken to her daughter very seriously indeed, and after much persuasion had succeeded in winning the coy maiden's consent. Would I come to a quiet family dinner that evening? The other dear girls would forgive and forget, and would receive me as a brother.

"Pleading a bad headache I declined the old lady's invitation, and during the remainder of the week I strenuously avoided meeting any member of the family. I kept what had passed strictly to myself, not even unburdening my soul to Rochester, and I fondly hoped that I should receive ' Jo's ' release without the matter coming to the ears of the Colonel. But, in spite of my reticence, disquieting rumours reached the Regiment, and fluttered about the ante-room, for Mrs. Puckerow was so proud of her first spoil that she spread the news of her daughter's engagement far and wide, and my hesitating replies to the point-blank questions of my friends served only to confirm the damaging reports. But as yet the fatal fact was unknown to my Commanding Officer. By pure chance I ran up against ' Jo ' one evening at the band-stand, and shortly afterwards I found myself walking with her confidentially down a side-path of the gardens.

" ' I think you treat me very badly, considering how I have helped you out of your difficulties,' began ' Jo ' with a pout.

" ' Why, Miss Puckerow, what am I to do ?' I replied, beginning to feel uncomfortable.

"'When a girl is engaged,' said 'Jo' dogmatically, 'she expects the man to show her a little kindness, doesn't she?'

"'Ye—es, yes, quite so; but you see, don't you know, really and truly you and I are not quite what you may call exactly engaged, are we?'

"'Indeed, but we *are*, most regularly engaged. It is true I have kindly undertaken to let you off—in time; but until I do so, please remember that we are an engaged couple, and unless you treat me very nicely, perhaps I shall not part with you after all.'

"After this terrible threat I saw that I must mind my stops, or I should find myself in worse trouble than ever. Then followed a long conversation, in the course of which we came to terms; they were these:—1. I was publicly to give out the engagement. 2. I was to send her a ring. 3. I was to call at the Web, and take her for a ride three times a week. 4. I was to walk with her every band-night. 5. I was to call her Mary, and was to be called by her Marmaduke. These were the conditions imposed upon *me*. On her part she merely renewed the covenant of release, of which the time, place, and manner were to be left entirely to her good will and pleasure. It is needless to say that from that moment the news ran

about the station like wild-fire, and in the course
of the following day I was summoned to the
Colonel's quarters.   I will not attempt to describe
that   animated   interview.   Colonel   Harde's
language in the quietest of times was forcible,
grandly forcible, but on this occasion he was
roused to the most tempestuous passion, and his
rhetoric, I assure you, nearly blew the roof off.
He did all the talking.   I never had a look in, and
after the worst twenty minutes I ever experienced,
I left the house like a toad escaping from a red-
hot harrow, and when I recovered my scattered
senses all that I could recollect of this pulverizing
interview was the frequently thundered adjuration
to exchange without delay into another Regiment.
From that moment the Colonel never let me
alone; I was the one object upon which he concentrated his wrath, scorn, and denunciation; he
bullied me on parade, derided me at mess, and
gibed at me in private society.   I was constantly
summoned to the orderly-room for faults so trivial
that in former days they either would not have
attracted his attention, or would have been
dismissed with a laugh.   In this state of affairs
it is needless to say that I sought about for an
exchange, in order that I might flee away and be
at rest.

"About this period a new Civil swell came to the station. He was a commissioner, or a tax-collector, I forget what they called him, but he drew over three thousand rupees a month, and lived in the biggest house in the place, so he must have been a boss of sorts. This gentleman at once began to make up to 'Jo.' He had met her the year before up at Pindi, and I heard afterwards that he had paid her a good deal of attention there. After his arrival I found my treaty engagements sensibly relaxing. First 'Jo' knocked off the morning rides, soon she remitted the evening walks, then she dropped the 'Marmaduke,' and finally I received a note from her mother returning me the engagement-ring, and saying that it had at last become clear to her daughter that, owing to the disparity of our ages, and the incompatibility of our tempers, we should never be happy together; she therefore released me from my pledges. The letter concluded by asking me to come over that evening to a quiet dinner. Under this was written in 'Jo's' hand, 'Better not,' and scrawled across the envelope in pencil by the same writer was added as though by an after-thought, 'Never say that I don't keep my word!'"

"What luck!" ejaculated Snapper, who had

L

been listening breathlessly to the recital, "out of danger at last."

"Well, to tell you the truth, it was then that my most imminent danger began, for I felt, now that I had lost her, that I cared for Mary Puckerow a very considerable deal, so much so that I at once ordered my horse, intending to gallop over to the Web, and swear that I would never give her up, and, in fact, would marry her right away. Just as I was mounting, Rochester and some other fellows rode up and summoned me to a pig-sticking expedition; they would take no excuse, and escape was impossible. Being half mad with vexation I rode a bit wild, and going at a gallop over some blind ground my horse fell into a nullah, pitching me on to my head. I was taken home senseless, and for six weeks was confined to my bed. When I got about again I heard that 'Jo' had married the tax-collector, and had left the station. Matters having thus adjusted themselves, my application for an exchange was withdrawn, and I was re-admitted to the Colonel's favour. But to this day I have never been able quite to satisfy myself whether 'Jo' meant to run straight from start to finish in that affair or not. Heigh ho! who's for whist?"

A PANDOURADE.

————o————

"THAT was rather tall tipple which you gave the Gunners the other night, Colonel Bowlong," remarked Parkinson, one evening, a day or two after an unusually "wet" night at our mess. "A bit of a tickler, wasn't it!" replied our chief, complacently; "it was a favourite drink in the old Pandours."

"Was it peculiar to the Regiment, sir?"

"Yes, it was our own special brew. It was invented on the field of Ferozeshah. We were bivouacking during 'the night of horrors' in the midst of a Sikh battery that we had charged and taken in our usual topping style, and one of us having found a keg of brandy in a corner of an embrasure, we turned a kettle-drum into a punch-bowl and filled it with the spirit. Riding-Master Tipples produced a bottle of curaçoa from his left holster and a bunch of chillies from his right, and just as we had completed the brew a shell burst into the midst of us and set it alight. That was the origin of the celebrated Pandour Punch, otherwise known as 'Samson with his hair on,' and our first toast was to the memory of Tipples, who, I forgot to mention, received the shell where he had hoped to put the punch. Yes, it is a noble beverage, and was once a great favourite of mine. It gives me cold shivers now, it always makes me think of ghosts."

" Did you ever see a ghost, Colonel ? "

" Ay, thirty-one."

" What ! all at once, sir ? "

" All at once, and only once ; a second experience of the sort would have driven me mad."

We instinctively drew our chairs closer round our leader, for we saw that he was in the vein for history.

" How was it, Colonel ? Do you mind telling us the story ? "

" Well, it fell out in this way. About a year after the destruction of the old Pandours — I have often told you about that business—I was carrying despatches from Sir Hugh Rose to the Governor-General, and my route lay through Rowdibad, the station where our Regiment had been cantoned up to the outbreak of the Mutiny. Being quite alone, and knowing that the city, at the best of times a place of very evil repute, was seething with a fanatical and highly excitable

rebel population, I determined to avoid the town
and to seek shelter for the night in the old cavalry
mess-house, which lay in the midst of the now
ruined and deserted cantonments, about a mile and
a half from the city. The last rays of the sun
were disappearing as I rode into the building—no
difficult feat, for every door in the place had been
torn from its hinges, and there was no furniture
to get in one's way. The only room with a roof
remaining to it was the great dining-room, which
I had known in former days so full of life and
comfort, but which now confronted me in all the
hideousness of ruin that has not had time to
assume the picturesque adjuncts of age. As I
entered the room a jackal rushed past me,
resenting what he evidently considered an un-
warrantable intrusion upon his lair, and a cloud
of bats, disturbed by the clatter of my horse's
hoofs upon the boards, flew round and round, flap-
ping and twittering. Tethering my horse to an
old hook that in former days had helped to support
a wall-lamp, I wrapped myself in my cloak and
lay down as supperless as my nag. While I
lay waiting for sleep, my mind was busy with
reflections of the past. I conjured up the various
scenes of jollity that I had taken part in within
those now deserted walls; I thought of the gay

dances, the uproarious banquets, and all the roystering revelry of the wild, old days; then I reflected upon the fate of my old friends and comrades. Of those who, a year or two before, had filled these rooms with life and gaiety, there was hardly a man or a woman that was not now lying in a bloody grave! To-night was the anniversary of the battle of Ferozeshah, when we charged the great battery and saved the day. We were justly proud of that exploit, and always celebrated it by an annual dinner, and a tremendous sky-lark after mess. It was an episode in a man's life to have dined with the Pandours on a Ferozeshah-night. 'Ah! those mad times have passed away for ever,' I said to myself; 'tame enough are the limbs that took part in the Bedlam pranks and pandemonium war-dances; tame enough till they rally to the last trumpet.'

"*Tarára—tarára—tará—tará—tarárará!* It was a distinct cavalry call, and was sounded in the compound, just outside the door. Springing to my feet I disengaged my horse and mounted, for I thought that I was in for a night gallop with half the Gwalior contingent at my heels; but imagine my astonishment when I perceived the room gradually lighting up until it was nearly as bright as day. I then saw that things were in exactly the same condition as on the night when I last dined there; the room was carpeted with the same old double pile, the walls were furnished with the usual array of lamps, the long table, white with snowy linen, gleamed with glass and flashed brightly with gold and silver plate. Again the trumpet sounded, and I knew it now to be the call for mess.. With the last note of the cadence the doors flew open, and the Colonel, old Lashem Harde, rode slowly in; he was in the full dress of the Regiment, busby, sword and all, and was mounted upon an enormous gaunt black charger, with flaming eyes, a heavy mane, and a sweeping tail; close behind him rode the two Majors, followed by the Captains, Lieutenants and Cornets, the regimental staff bringing up the rear, all being mounted upon huge black skeleton chargers, with glowing eyes and tremendous manes and tails. The officers looked neither to right nor left, but moved in solemn procession after the Colonel. Harde led them at a slow march three times round the room, and then all fell into their places at the table, the Colonel in his old position in the centre. I observed that the company did not quite fill up the table, and that there was one blank space. A growing horror seized me as I realized that the vacant place was mine. Indeed,

I at first felt a powerful inclination to ride round
and occupy it, but I wrestled with and overcame
the sinister prompting. Four mess-servants now
entered, staggering under the weight of what
appeared to be an enormous brazen bowl of
blazing punch, which, by a tremendous effort, they
hoisted on to the table in front of the Colonel.
It was the old Ferozeshah kettle-drum, but
greatly magnified. The servants then brought
trays covered with curious old goblets, the
handles of which, I noticed, were wrought into the
semblance of writhing and inter-twisted imps. In
a moment, by a process so swift that I was unable
to follow it with the eye, each man's hand grasped
one of these quaint vessels filled to the brim with
the flaming liquid. The Colonel, in a voice that
rang through the room and echoed among the
rafters, gave the order to draw swords, and as the
warriors sat with their faces flashing in the light of
the flaring goblets and the gleaming swords, they
presented a spectacle that I am thankful to think
the eye of man but seldom rests upon.

"The Colonel now shouted for a song; his voice
was sepulchrally deep, and there was a harsh,
defiant, but at the same time despairing, ring about
it that sent a chill to my very marrow. But this
sensation was surpassed in horror by that which

followed. The effect of the deafening notes of the devil's ditty into which the assembly burst is simply indescribable ; the sound was the very voice of Gehenna ; through the song one heard every scale and key and semi-tone of pain ; the hearer felt that the singers were overborne by a despair beyond the conception of a finite brain, while the whole movement was accompanied by an undertone of hideous forced hilarity that presented a revolting discord to the prevailing movement of lamentation and regret. At the end of each verse the singers clashed their swords together savagely and took a deep draught of the liquid fire. The words of the demon doggrel were something like these :—

    " ' Who knows the fate that waits him here ?
                  Ha ha !
   ' Pest, disaster, bullet, spear,
                  Tra la !
   ' To death, whichever course we take,
                  Life wends.
   ' All's one—but mark—in death we wake !
                  Sleep ends.
   ' We wake to add the reckoning up,
[A low moaning]
   ' To drink a never-emptied cup,'

[Here the voices burst into a brief tempestuous roar of demoniac violence]

> ' What lies behind the sable veil ?
>   I trow
> ' Brain would reel and heart would quail
>   To know.'

[The song now reached its wildest pitch of intensity, frantic screams arose on all sides, and I felt as though my head must burst if the ditty lasted much longer]

> ' Now we read the riddle well,
> ' Here the secret we may tell,
> ' And howl the mysteries of ——'

" At this moment the Colonel's glance fell upon me, and with an abrupt wave of his sabre he stopped the singing.

" ' A life,' he thundered, ' a life, a soul ! ' and he leapt his great charger towards me over the mess-table.

" The whole company, as though moved by electricity, immediately made for me ; some came round at a gallop, others cleared the table, as though it were a mere riding-school jump, and those that were nearest to me made their great animals wheel and face me. In a second I was surrounded by a circle of merciless, menacing faces. They were the countenances of the men with whom I had for years lived on terms of intimacy and good fellowship, but in not one of those deeply-suffering, desperate faces could I read the slightest trace of human kindness or friendly recognition, and I now knew, what I had before only feared, that the beings pressing so savagely around me were souls of the lost. I looked from one to the other and recognized them all. But what a change, fearful though undefinable, had fallen upon them! The first man that I noticed was Charlie Rochester, in life the cheeriest of companions, but the most pitiless of *roués*. I will not attempt to describe that man's appearance. I once found a very near approach to it in a quotation from Andante."

"Dante, wasn't it, Colonel?" whispered the Doctor; "he describes people of that sort in the 'Inferno.'"

"I refer to the fellow that wrote 'Paradise Lost,'" replied the Colonel, with some degree of hauteur; "but my memory is not good for those things, and I can't give you the exact words. The next man whom I observed was Venager, the duellist, the man whose name had been a terror to every station in which he had been quartered. He used to boast that he had given more work to the monument-makers than any other man in the army, and that there was not a grave-yard near which he had been stationed that he had not handsomely contributed to.   This man used to pick quarrels and kill men for the mere lust of butchery; to my own knowledge he had destroyed twenty-seven of his opponents on the ground; how many he had sent away mortally wounded or crippled for life I don't remember, and, mind you, I knew him only at the close of his career.   The shape before me still wore its old look of keen, murderous malice, reminding me how persistently the victim he had marked down would be followed up for a thoughtless act, a chance word, or even an unconsidered glance, until he was hunted into a corner from which there lay no escape save by sword or pistol.   Venager preferred the latter weapon, but he was perfection at both. In his pistol-duels his favourite object of aim had been the head, in his sword-fights the heart.   He used to say:—'I like clean killing; the head and the heart are the only parts worth a curse; plug the brain and save your powder, or tap the ventricle and save your time!'   A very unpleasant person was Venager, but we always treated him with re-spect.   The only man who ever had him properly 'on toast' was myself.   I'll tell you the story some day.

"Well, Venager presented a truly awful appear-ance; his haggard face, from chin to forehead, was

now so riddled with bullet-holes that it looked like
a Turk's head after an hour's very straight car-
bine-practice, and his frogged and braided coat,
where it covered his left breast, was pierced with
stabs and drenched with blood. Close by Venager
was Macflint, the man who spent all his money
at cards and on the turf, leaving his wife and
child at home to starve—literally to starve. The
fellow had three thousand a year, and his wife and
daughter perished in a London garret for want of
a crust of bread. Macflint, a *gourmé* and *gour-
mand* of the first water, was in life heavy and
obese, but the form before me was that of a man
suffering the acutest tortures of famine; his
sunken cheeks, his restless, wolfish eyes, his claw-
like hands, and his skeleton body, which, though
clothed in uniform, disclosed the sharp outline of
fleshless bones beneath, long afterwards haunted
me. The Colonel, who had been the most merciless martinet in the Service, kept moving his
shoulders shiftily as though writhing in ceaseless
pain, and I had little doubt that his back was
lacerated with the stripes that he had unjustly
inflicted upon many an honest soldier. But I had
no time for further scrutiny, for the circle had
closed upon me, a ring of gauntleted hands eagerly
proffering the blazing quaighs.

" ' Drink, sir ! ' thundered the Colonel. ' Drink, truant and poltroon, take your place in the ranks, and complete the complement ! ' and a wild demoniacal chorus of ' Drink, drink ! ' resounded through the room.

" The sound reverberated in my ears like the roar of Niagara, and the heat of the reeking goblets burnt my face like the flames of Etna. But I determinedly resisted all attempts to force upon me what I was now assured would make me free of this devil's guild. Both I and my horse were as though struck by catalepsy, neither of us could move a muscle, so any attempt to escape was out of the question. A dead silence fell upon my persecutors as they waited for me to yield, the only sound audible being the hissing and bubbling of the beverage that seethed around me in a ring of flame. For fully ten minutes I sat like one in a nightmare, encompassed by these accursed apostles of perdition, each mute as death, but with his gleaming eyes fixed upon me in ferocious expectation.

" ' Out with his heart ! ' suddenly roared Lashem, ' out with his heart and give it a hell-peg ! '

Straightway a dozen swords were plunged into my side, and in an instant my live and throbbing heart, spitted on a lurid blade, was handed to the

Colonel. He tossed part of the contents of his goblet at it, but the falling fire divided before it reached the palpitating organ, and fell in flaming streams upon the floor. With a bitter execration he tried again; but still the flame divided, and a third attempt was equally fruitless.

"'Too good for me,' bellowed the Chief; 'you try it, Major,' and he passed on the weapon.

"The Senior Major made the attempt, once, twice, and thrice, but with no better result; neither was the Junior Major more successful. Each failure evoked a burst of horrible blasphemy from the rest, every man of whom had three trials, but the fire shrank from the proffered sacrifice as though repelled by the protecting influence of an unseen power. The floor round our horses' hoofs was now a bath of lambent flame, but not a drop of the hell-broth had touched my poor heart, which at first, indeed, pulsated wildly with terror, but, as each successive attempt proved fruitless, soon resumed its normal composure.

"'Back with it!' thundered old Harde, with a blood-curdling anathema; 'he isn't one of us.'

"As he spoke, I saw a curious change come over his face; the expression was one of hungry, wolfish envy. I looked at the others, some were as the Colonel, others were wrathful and disappointed;

as for Venager, he was transfigured into the very genius of fury. He made as though he would charge me and cut me down, but though he spurred his horse savagely, some restraining energy was at work and held him back.

"'Rake-hells, a toast!' roared Lashem, who had now recovered his old air of supremacy.

"'A toast!' they all yelled, and again some occult action filled their goblets to the brim.

"The fiends turned their fiery eyes upon their leader, awaiting his next words.

"'*Bowlong, when he's ready ! ! !*'

"And amid a tempest of howls and curses the infernal crew tossed off the flaming potion. When comparative silence was restored, the Colonel, standing up in his stirrups and raising his voice to a higher pitch than ever, thus addressed the assembly :—

"'Let me remind you, gentlemen, of the occasion that brings us together this festive midnight. Officers of the Pandours, we meet to celebrate the anniversary of the ever-glorious victory of Ferozeshah, gained for the British Army by the immortal gallantry of the Pandour Hussars. Hip, hip, Hurra-a-h ! ! !'

"As he led the cheer he drove his charger violently against the Senior Major, at the same

time dealing that officer a tremendous back-
hander across the face with his sabre. The
Major turned fiercely upon the Colonel and
executed cut No. Seven with all his might upon his
Chief's busby. Upon this every one attacked his
nearest neighbour with the utmost fury; men
shouted in pain and anger, their horses snorted in
terror, blades clashed, pistols exploded, and in the
heat of the *mêlée* the great table was overturned
and the lamps were swept from the walls, reducing
the room to its pristine darkness. The weird
combat, however, raged more fiercely than ever in
the gloom. I now observed that when a horse was
spurred a shower of sparks flew from his side, and
whenever one of the combatants received a thrust
or a slash a stream of fire gushed from the wound;
the eyes, too, both of men and horses glowed like
live coals, and their breath was tinged with lurid
light. When the uproar was at its wildest the
trumpet suddenly sounded for the third time, and
the Colonel's voice rang out clear and distinct
above the tumult :—

" 'Officers of the Pandours, steady! Halt,
return swords, threes right, gallop mar-r-rch
to——'

The last word was drowned in the clatter of
the horses' hoofs as the accursed troop swept

M

like a whirlwind from the building. As the rear
section left the room a flash of lightning
illuminated the doorway, disclosing the cruel
bleeding face of Venager turned in my direction,
with a smile of such concentrated hate and con-
fident anticipation of future vengeance that my
brain, already strained beyond endurance, whirled
like a catherine-wheel, and I tumbled fainting on
the floor. As I rolled under the table there flashed
upon my mind a passing recollection of early
days, but the next instant I was unconscious.

" I rose at the earliest flush of dawn, and by the
light of a few matches I carefully examined the
apartment. It was just as I had found it on my
arrival the night before, gaunt, bare, and empty,
and it presented not the faintest indication of the
appalling scene that had been enacted there only
a few hours ago. Mounting my horse, I hurried
away in the growing light, and never again set eyes
on Rowdibad.

" It was not until a year after this episode that
our troops fairly reduced the neighbourhood to
order. The first night that our people occupied
the town a Major Fitz-Hopkins took up his quarters
in the old mess-house ; the next morning his corpse
was dragged out of the ruins. There had been a
fearful thunderstorm during the night, in the midst

of which the building had collapsed; but what puzzled everybody was that poor Fitz-Hopkins evidently was not killed by the fall, for the only injury discoverable was a wound in the throat, caused, so the doctors declared, by the action of fire. It was generally ascribed to lightning. I may, however, observe that the date of this occurrence was the anniversary of the battle of Feroze-shah.

"A year or two after this, finding myself in Rome, I related the story to my friend the Venerable and Illustrious Cardinal Sortello Annibelli, who, for many years, until expressly forbidden by the Pope, had applied himself to the study of demonology and the black art. I asked the Cardinal how it was that the fiends were so completely foiled in their efforts to consume my heart, and I put it to him as an ecclesiastic, whether it was incumbent upon me to attach any importance to their blood-curdling toast, which I confess had at times caused me some little anxiety. My venerable friend replied that the case was a very simple one; the Regiment, when it was hurled out of existence, was one man short of its strength of officers, and was serving its penance with that man, as it were, seconded; there was no doubt about it that the absentee was myself;

and the spirits, failing to secure their comrade, had got hold of the unfortunate Fitz-Hopkins. Their work on earth being then over, they destroyed the arena of their godless revelries. The failure to set fire to my heart, the Cardinal opined, was due to three causes, the first, my exemplary purity of life; the second, my consistent piety; and the third, and chief, my scrupulous nicety with regard to truth. 'Maintain these virtues,' said His Eminence, 'and you may laugh at the devil and his legions; but,' he added with impressive earnestness, 'mark me, *caro* Bologno, Signor Fitz-Hopkin' is only doing duty, and should you fall away in any one of the three particulars that I have enumerated, I cannot guarantee that you may not have to fall in with your old Regiment on the day of the last roll-call.'"

THE COLONEL'S DUEL.

——o——

ONE evening we reminded our Chief of the promised account of his quarrel with Captain Venager. "Oh, that stupid business," smiled the Colonel. "Well, I suppose I must tell you about it; but, mind you, I am in no degree an advocate for duelling. It was to that accursed practice that society owed such a scourge as Arnold Venager.

"My quarrel with him arose in this way: I was telling them at mess of a curious incident which had occurred during that afternoon, while I was out snipe-shooting. The occurrence was rather a curious one, and excited some little surprise; I had bagged a snipe, a hare, and a bustard at a single shot, but without hitting any one of them. It happened like this: a snipe and a bustard rose together, the snipe flying from me, and the bustard crossing the snipe's bows from right to left; the bustard was a long shot for number nine, so I fired at the snipe. Simultaneously with the report, I saw through the smoke the bustard falling head-

long to the ground. On picking him up I found
lying under him a hare with its neck broken.
Examining the bustard, I saw tucked under his
left wing the snipe, with its bill driven well home
into the big bird's heart. The three were as dead
as a door-nail, but deuce a pellet had struck any
one of 'em. It was simple enough when explained.
The snipe had speared the bustard, killing itself
by the shock, and the bustard had crushed the
hare. No reasonable man would have found anything in such a simple narrative to cavil at; the
only incredible part of it was my missing the
snipe; but Venager saw fit to doubt the story.
He burst into a roar of laughter, and then in his
most offensive manner asked :

"'Why did you not say the snipe had drilled a
hole in an elephant, it would make a better tale?'
At this there was a general laugh, and I felt a bit
uncomfortable.

"'I don't introduce an elephant into the story,'
I answered, ' because it would be at variance with
the facts.'

Venager smiled significantly and said : ' Faith !
and that would be a trifle—*for you !* '

" Matters now began to look serious; he was
evidently bent upon fastening a quarrel upon
me.

"'What do you mean by that?' I asked, looking him straight in the eyes.

"Venager now assumed his fighting scowl, and replied so loudly that he was heard by every man at the table:

"'I mean simply this, Mr. Bowlong, that the fables which you see proper so frequently to regale us with are fit only for the pages of'"—here the Colonel looked unutterably solemn, and lowered his voice to a tragic whisper—"'of Baron Munchausen!' and slowly draining his glass, the speaker rose and sauntered from the room.

"For a moment there was a profound silence, a sudden chill had settled upon every one but myself; not a man there but looked upon me as one already lying encased upon a gun-carriage; for it was clear, after what had passed, I had no option but to send Venager a challenge. Three or four fellows near me tried to revive the conversation, but the effort was lame and futile; the only man totally unconcerned was myself, and I felt that it rested with me to infuse gaiety into the company, so I called for champagne, and sending it round, I got up and, in my cheeriest manner, proposed my own health and my opponent's destruction. As the applause died away, we heard the wheels of Venager's buggy going out of the compound. It was his practice before a duel to retire to bed early; late hours unsteadied his hand. After mess I retired to a quiet corner of the ante-room, and there composed what was, in those days, called a hostile message. I had no difficulty about that; the youngest subaltern who might have blundered over accepting an invitation to dinner, knew well enough how to write a challenge. My embarrassment, however, began when I tried to secure a messenger. I wandered round the room, letter in hand, dropping down confidentially first by one, then by another of my friends, but not a man of them could I induce to carry the cartel. I did not know till afterwards that, while I was writing my defiance, word went quickly round the room to refuse to assist either Venager or myself in carrying our quarrel to extremes. It was known that mediation with my opponent was out of the question, intercession on my behalf would have been about as effective as a plea to a tiger in favour of a lamb; but we could not fight without seconds, so a strict neutrality was agreed to by all. Failing to secure a messenger, I dropped the letter into the station post-office, and calmly waited the result. No sooner had Venager received my message, than he hastily sought a friend to convey his reply, and to administer to me a severe wigging for the insolent irregularity of which I had been guilty in presuming to forward a challenge by post. But my enemy was as unsuccessful in his quest as I had been in mine. Not a man in the Regiment would support either the one or the other of us. You see the real fact was that the fellows did not want to see me killed. There were no officers in the station but ourselves; the Mutiny was brewing, and the remainder of our brigade had been sent by forced marches to Meerut, where we were daily expecting orders to follow them. Here, for the first time in his life, Venager met with a check, for it was altogether opposed to Pandour principles to admit civilians to a share in regimental quarrels. But he was checked only for a moment; nothing was allowed to foil that man in his appetite for human blood.

"In the matter of a second, my antagonist succeeded no better than I had done, and after having tried the fellows all round without success, and having been on the verge of a quarrel with more than half of them in consequence, he sent me his reply by a mounted orderly. Of course, my challenge was accepted, gleefully accepted; and the weapon chosen was the straight cavalry sword. There the matter rested for the present. Venager meant to kill me, and therefore dared not fight without witnesses—his record was so bad, that if he had pinked me in a corner, things might have gone precious hard with him. We used to meet every day at mess, and it was amazing to see the constrained air of courtesy that the duellist now assumed towards me. In all duelling matters he was a purist for punctilio, and he displayed the same ceremony towards a man whom he intended to kill as a heathen priest does to the object of his sacrifice. I caught his eye, though, more than once fixed on a spot on my waistcoat, a little to the left of the third button, and, as I read his thoughts, my reflections were not altogether exhilarating. But I kept my head up, and put on an appearance of indifference—for in these and all other matters where men contend together it gives your opponent too much of a pull over you to let him think that you funk him. But all the fellows looked upon me as a doomed man ; sooner or later we should find ourselves again cantoned with other troops, and then there would be seconds in plenty —sixty a minute, ha, ha ! But Venager was growing impatient at the delay, he became restless and feverish, his appetite failed, he complained to the doctor that he could not sleep, and his health was evidently becoming affected by his balked desire to contribute me to the Rowdibad cemetery. One

evening, after a long day with the duck, I was
riding back to cantonments a little late for dinner.
As I passed the station racket-court I heard some
one hailing me from the porch.

" ' Mr. Bowlong, a word with you.'

" I recognized Venager's voice, and pulled up.
He came forward, and said haughtily,—

" ' The route has come. We march for Meerut at
nine o'clock. There is some fighting to be done at
Delhi—life in a campaign being uncertain, I propose that we settle our differences before starting.
I have been waiting for you since four o'clock. In
half an hour the moon will be up, and we can
fight in the racket-court without disturbance.
Unfortunately we have no witnesses, but that
we cannot help. I have brought the weapons,'
and he held out two sabres.

" I chose one, and silently followed him into
the building. We ascended the narrow stairs that
led into the gallery, and sat down to await the
rising of the moon. Venager seated himself as
far from me as possible—his way, I suppose, of
letting me know that, for the present, he desired
no further communication with me. On the
bench where I had settled myself, some one had
left a cigar-case, which, from its size, I knew
belonged to Batiscombe, our Junior Major. Frank

Idstone Batiscombe was popularly understood to consume his own length in cheroots daily, and his magazine was of the size and strength of a small portmanteau. I was glad to find that the case was full; selecting one I struck a match, and by its light I perceived Venager's evil eyes fixed on the corner where I was sitting. It was too dark to see me, but he kept his gaze on my position, like a wild beast whose instinct tells him through the darkness of midnight where the prey is lying.

" ' Have a cheroot ? ' I asked, as cheerfully as I could, ' I've found Batiscombe's case.'

" There was a pause, and then came the reply.

" ' I never smoke on these occasions, sir, and I would advise you rather to occupy the next few minutes in prayer, than to devote them to the indulgence of boyish bravado.'

" I felt sat upon, but went on with my cheroot all the same, and as I smoked I reflected that I was about to do a very foolish thing. I was going to encounter the best swordsman in the army, and the most unscrupulous man in Asia, I was going to fight by moonlight and without seconds. That Venager intended to kill me I had not the slightest doubt, and that he would not be over nice in his way of doing it was abundantly clear from all the attendant circumstances. The Regiment was moving to the front; in a day or two it would be engaged in a stormy campaign; no one would have time or opportunity to inquire what had become of me; and the station being left without any European, my bones would bleach before any one visited the racket-court; and as I pictured myself a corpse lying locked away from the world, exposed to sun and shower, vulture and crow, I confess I winced a bit.

"'Here's the moon,' said Venager, with a sigh of relief, as the great silver orb tipped the back wall and shed a flood of radiance into the court. 'If you have no objection we will go down.'

"I stumbled down the dark staircase and entered the court, closely followed by Venager, who immediately shut and locked the door, putting the key in his pocket.

"'Now, sir,' he said, in a fierce whisper, as he took up his position in the centre of the court, where the moonlight fell clearest.

"My antagonist, having bowed to me with much ceremony, performed the usual fencing - school salutations with scrupulous exactness, and as I clumsily followed suit I could not avoid being forcibly struck by the lissom grace of all his movements, which in their sinuous complexity resembled the artless undulation of a serpent rather than the studied action of a human being. At last our blades met, and I had crossed swords with the most formidable duellist of the age. And now my eyes beheld such a sight of horror as to turn my nerves to ice. The features of the man in front of me had suddenly set into the mask of an old Greek fury, growing so hideously distorted with the rage of combat that the appearance of them will remain branded upon my mental retina for ever. His big black eyes glowed with more than feline fire; his lips were drawn tightly back, exposing under his scant black moustache the close-set white teeth gleaming in the moonlight; his hard square chin protruded savagely, like the muzzle of a beast of prey; his hair, which, after the fashion of those days, was long, lay in tangled masses upon his high, narrow forehead, and the whole face gloomed with the scowl of murder. I could hear the wild beast writhing within him in the ravenous grinding of his teeth, and the hoarse half-smothered curses that were hurled forth as though shot from a volcano of blasphemy within. In a moment the truth flashed upon me, and I knew the secret of Venager's hideous career. The man was *mad*—and there was I, poor Pilgarlic, cut off from all assistance, shut up at night within the

four walls of a lonely racket-court, in company
with an armed and hostile homicidal maniac. A
maniac, but one so skilful in the manipulation of
every weapon that no man had yet been found
able to stand before him and live. The situation
was certainly fraught with both difficulty and
danger, and, moreover, I freely admit, was not
unattended with some degree of anxiety. But
you must not think that I was exactly in the
position of a sheep before the slaughterer. I had
learnt fencing in France, and though as an all-
round swordsman I was but a child in the hands
of such a man as Venager, I possessed the knowledge of one manœuvre that I felt sure would
astonish him. My old *maître d'armes* had taught
me a thrust—the *coup de Grisier*—devised by himself and called by his own name : it was a sort of
half - arm *riposte* delivered as your adversary
attacked in tierce, like this——" and as the narrator described the movement with a dessert-fork
upon a mango, it seemed certainly to possess in
an eminent degree the merit of simplicity. Laying down his fork with a complacent smile, the
Colonel sipped his claret and resumed :—

"You thus struck your antagonist in the centre
of the funny-bone and completely disabled him ;
in fact, if sent well home the blow might be relied

upon to prevent his ever using his sword again, at any rate with that arm, as long as he lived. But, of course, one had to wait till the man in front exposed himself. . Well, Venager, after waiting for an instant, made a trial-pass at me, which I parried in excellent form. This seemed to surprise him, for he apparently had regarded me as a tyro. He then began to edge away to my left front, disengaging as he moved, but at each disengage I countered and turned with him. For a few moments I began indeed to think that if I remained strictly on the defensive I might perhaps hold my own. But the hope was soon rudely dispelled. Suddenly, like an arrow shot from a strong steel bow, my opponent's sword leapt over my guard and struck me with tremendous force just over the heart. But, strange to say, instead of finding myself transfixed upon the blade, I felt only the slightest prick of the point. I was too much confused by the rapidity of the movement to try my cherished *coup*, and in the fraction of a second, Venager had recovered his guard and was looking curiously at me surprised, I supposed, that I did not fall in a pool of blood. But seeing that I was not yet what the French call *une quantité négligeable*, he again began working away to the left, and once more, like a shock of electricity, came the blow, straight as a line, for my pericardium. Again I felt the puncture as it were of a needle, but nothing more. If it had not been for the smart, I should have thought that my opponent had a button on his sword; but a moment's reflection would have told me that such a supposition with respect to Arnold Venager was extravagant to absurdity. After a feint or two at my right shoulder he again drove his weapon, quick as thought, against my left breast, repeating the attack with apparent success again and again, but, to his evident perplexity and to my bewildered joy, his efforts resulted in nothing more effective than would have been the case if he had been using a blunted foil. It is true that now and again I felt the slight pricking sensation that I have already described, but I was satisfied that as yet I had received no wound. At last I became accustomed to his mode of attack, and as he was lunging at me for the seventh time, I succeeded in accomplishing the Grisier *coup*. The result was magical, his arm dropped as though struck by a bullet, and his sword fell with a clang upon the concrete. In half a second I had picked up his weapon and tossed it over the wall.

"I could hardly believe my senses, Venager the invincible was conquered. The change wrought

N

upon my antagonist by this unexpected termination of our encounter was remarkable. For the first time in his turbulent career he found himself at another man's mercy, and though a determined and persistent duellist, he was not altogether reckless of his life. In all his contests he had felt himself so immeasurably superior to those he fought with that a duel made no great demand upon his courage. At last a fitting test of his fortitude had arrived, how would he acquit himself? His fury at once vanished, and not a trace of excitement was now perceptible. He stood before me cool, collected, and serene, and I could see that he had completely recovered his usual haughty self-confidence. He was moving towards the door, but I barred the way with the point of my sword.

"'Why! what are you going to do?' he asked, amazed at my interposition.

"'Our quarrel is not going to end like this,' said I, placing the point of my sword against his waistcoat.

"'Don't for a moment dream that I will apologize to you, if that is what you mean; and have the goodness to remove your sword,' said he, with a menacing look.

"'I will dispense with the formality of an apology,' I replied, 'but I trust that you will recognize the necessity of complying with my desire in another matter?'

"'*Necessity* is a strong word,' he sneered. 'Well, state your desire,' and he carelessly attempted to bind up his bleeding elbow with a handkerchief, of which he held one end between his teeth.

"'Up in the gallery yonder,' I replied, 'you very considerately recommended me to say my prayers. I did so, and with the result that you have now experienced. May I retort the request upon you?'

"'What in the world do you mean?' he inquired, loftily.

"'I mean that you shall kneel down here and pray for the souls of all those unfortunate men that you have hurried into an untimely grave.'

"'Go to the d——l!' was the contemptuous reply.

"'I shall certainly be under the painful necessity of sending you to him,' said I, 'unless you at once do as I have requested you.' He was evidently startled at the firmness of my tone; but still his predominant feeling was anger.

"'Do you think that because you have, by the merest accident, come off best on this one occasion, you can presume to take an attitude of compulsion with *me!!* Have a care, young gentleman; believe me, you are treading on very dangerous ground.

N 2

If you were prudent you would solicit my pardon for provoking me to parade you, and would hasten to acknowledge the gross absurdity of your account of that adventure with the birds,' and he again tried to pass by me to the door. But I resolutely warned him back.

"'Captain Venager, time presses, down on your knees and make supplication for your victims, or my sword shall pierce you as assuredly as the snipe's bill transfixed the bustard,' and I put myself on guard with a tragic flourish. Venager started with indignation at this fresh instance of my audacity.

"'By the powers that made you,' he cried, in threatening accents, 'before the week is out I will teach you, Mr. Bowlong, such a lesson as will make you wish that you had never been born!' and he shook his left fist furiously.

"My reply to this menace was a fierce thrust at his chest, which he avoided only by quickly stepping backwards.

"'Would you murder me, you infernal scoundrel!' he shouted, as I followed him slowly up towards the back wall.

"'You know full well,' said I, bitterly, 'that you brought me here with the deliberate intention of murdering *me*—no doubt under the cover of conventional forms, but of murdering me never-theless. Now, sir, what is to prevent my dropping you where you stand, and saying it was done in fair fight, to which you forced me. Here are your own swords to bear me out, and there is no wit-ness to disprove the statement. By heaven! to kill you would be as meritorious as to shoot a tiger or to crush a cobra. Down on your knees, vampire, and pray for your murdered dead, or I drive my weapon home!'

"All the time that I had been speaking I had continued to advance upon him, until I had forced him, pallid and trembling with impotent rage, into a corner. Of course, I could not kill an unarmed man, but I pretended to be as ruthless a ruffian as my antagonist, and such is the effect of an evil conscience that he believed me to be in earnest.

"'Hold hard, you young madman,' he cried, as I brought my sword's point within a hair's breadth of his throat, 'what, in the name of folly, is it that you want?'

"'Kneel,' I repeated, in my sternest accents, 'and repeat what I tell you.' As I spoke I drew back my sword and made as though his death would be the immediate result of further hesitation. For an instant he wavered; he was balancing the chances of a sudden spring and a struggle, but my point was in a line with his throat, and behind him was the wall; the odds were hopelessly against him, and seeing me rolling my eyes and displaying my teeth just as he himself had done during the fight, he thought he read his doom in my face, and with an awful imprecation, down he went on to his marrow-bones. Ye gods! what a sight for men and angels! How I regretted that some of the Regiment were not present to witness it. Arnold Venager, the destroyer, the pitiless tyrant whom all men feared and courted, down on his knees before the junior subaltern, and repeating a pious formula which that exemplary young person was carefully composing for his benefit. I made him pray first for poor Jack Richardson, then for Reginald Allaway, Clarence Payne, Dick Fitzmaurice, and as many more as I could recollect, some two dozen in all ; and then, hearing our trumpets in the barrack-square sounding the ' fall-in,' I lowered my sword and allowed my unwilling bedesman to get up. We left the court in silence. Outside in the moonlight stood our animals where we had tethered them. When Venager had mounted he turned to me, and growled :—' There is one soul that you forgot to offer prayers for, but which will require it before long.' As he sat bareheaded on his black seventeen-hand Australian, under the shadow of the trees, he looked like some demon huntsman in an enchanted forest.

"'Whose soul do you refer to?' I asked, as I scrambled on to my pony.

"'*Your own!*' he thundered, and wheeling his charger, he galloped headlong into the darkness.

"'That means *pistols* next time,' I reflected, 'and no *coup de Grisier* can help me at *that* game.' But I had little time to ponder future eventualities, my present and leading thought was how to get on to parade before the Regiment marched, so I spurred my pony and made full tilt for home. My charger was standing ready saddled at the door, belts, sword, and uniform lay on the cot, and in quicker time than I had ever before done it, I was on the parade-ground, following my Captain down the line. Luckily for me, Venager did not live to play the return match. Before the week was out he had fallen at the storming of Muzbutjak."

"But, Colonel, how do you account for your wonderful escape from those seven or eight thrusts that were made at you?" inquired the Doctor.

The Colonel's eye twinkled:—"Oh! I had forgotten to tell you about that part of the business. I owed my life, humanly speaking, to old Battiscombe's cigar-case, which I had thoughtlessly stuck into my breast-pocket. But it was mainly the monogram that saved me, for—and it proved the deadly accuracy of Venager's hand and eye—not a single blow had missed the metal, which, as chance had it, exactly covered and protected my heart. The leather opposite the characters was simply cut to ribbons, and the cheroots that lay between were chopped into chaff. As for the design itself, it was so hacked and twisted that Battiscombe actually failed to recognize his own initials! Indeed, few of those to whom I have shown this interesting relic have been able to detect in the tangle the letters 'F. I. B.'

" What's the joke, Doctor ? "

THE SECRET OF THE SNOWS.

—o—

SIR MUNDUS TROTTER, M.P., while on a cold-weather tour through India some years ago, spent a day or two at our station and dined one evening at the mess. He was an alert, vivacious little man, and eager for information upon all topics relating to India. During dinner the conversation turned upon the Sepoy Mutiny, and our guest expressed his surprise at the lack of authentic information relating to the fate of Nana Sahib.

" Jules Verne will tell you all about it," observed the Doctor, laughing.

" But that is fiction," interposed Colonel Bowlong, "and Sir Mundus is inquiring after fact."

" Quite so," said the visitor ; " and it is to my mind one of the most remarkable circumstances in history that the fate of a man whose deeds are so notorious should continue to be wrapped in mystery."

" His fate is *not* unknown, Sir Mundus," replied the Colonel, solemnly.

" Indeed, sir ! You surprise me," exclaimed the other. " Are you, then, acquainted with the secret ? "

" The end of that miscreant was known to only three people," continued the Colonel. " Two of them have gone to their long home—the third, sir, is now addressing you."

Sir Mundus slowly lowered the claret-glass that he was raising to his lips, and, adjusting a pair of gold *pince-nez* spectacles, turned towards the Colonel with a look of profound interest, mingled with growing personal respect.

" Were you, sir, then an actor in the closing scene of that tremendous drama, the opening of which was enacted at Cawnpore ? "

" In truth, I was," responded the Colonel with a sigh, as though the recollection came fraught with tragic memories.

" Might I, Colonel Bowlong, without undue pre-sumption, ask to be favoured with this momentous fragment of unwritten history ? To hear it would alone be worth a voyage to India."

" Shall we move into the verandah ? " said the Colonel, courteously, as he rose from the table ; " you may find me less prosy over a cigar."

All of us being comfortably settled in our favourite chairs, with our Manillas well aglow, the

Colonel spoke as follows :—" When Havelock made his first attempt to get to Lucknow, he left Neill and me in charge of his base at Cawnpore. As we two sat at dinner on the night of the General's departure, Neill said to me :—' Bowlong, my boy, I shall not die happy unless I know that the Bithoor butcher has had his ' kail through the reek.' Of course, *I* can't leave this post, but it is different with you. Marmaduke, you are the man to run him down. You shall have half a troop of cavalry and a lakh of rupees, and as much time as you like.'

" ' I'll do it, Jamie,' I said ; ' I shall not want the troopers, but I accept the time and the tin.'

" That was all that passed between us on the subject. Long before gun-fire next morning I was closeted with the high priest of the little temple by the Suttee Chowra Ghât. This man was a very slippery character. From his wonderful knack of betraying his friends and circumventing his enemies, he had for years been known among the natives by the name of ' *Burabalang*,' or the ' old Twister.' At the outbreak of the Mutiny he had attached himself to Sir Hugh Wheeler, and had repeatedly warned him against the Nana ; but finding the veteran deaf to his cautions, and foreseeing his own ruin in the

destruction that overhung the confiding British
community, he cast in his lot with the mutineers,
and thenceforward was one of Sir Hugh's most
dangerous enemies; then seeing the tide turning
with the approach of Havelock's column, he
promptly ratted from his rebel friends, and by
timely information of an important character
made his peace with the Sirkar, and had ever since
professed the strongest desire to assist us. He was
doubtless afraid that some ugly facts about the
massacre might crop up, and he thought it safest
to hedge. After a decent amount of beating about
the bush, I came to the point:—'Where is the
Nana?'

"'He is dead.'

"'How dead?'

"'Drowned, my lord, in the holy Ganges.'

"'Are you certain of that?'

"'*Huzoor*, did I not see him die?'

"'Where, and when?'

"'*Khudawund*, be not angry with me! On the
night that the victorious Havelock Bahadur drove
the rebel sons of dogs from Cawnpore, I procured
a boat, and taking it to Bithoor, received Nana
Punt at the landing-place. He entered the boat,
followed by a servant carrying a lantern; a crowd
of *Gunga Putras* had accompanied him to the ghât.

He gave them the blessing of a dying priest, saying with a loud voice :—' My sons, when this light is extinguished, I shall be in the arms of Mother Gunga.' We pushed off and rowed across the river, then the light was put out, and the Nana——'

" ' Stepped ashore, mounted a horse that was in readiness, and rode away,' said I, concluding the sentence.

" Burabalang looked at me with a terrified stare. He knew that it was deadly dangerous work playing fast and loose with James Neill.

" ' Come, was it not so ? ' I demanded, sharply.

" ' The nourisher of the poor knows everything,' muttered the Brahmin.

" ' There is *one* thing that I don't know, and that you must help me to discover, namely, the Nana's present hiding-place,' said I, trying to fix his shifty eyes.

" The Twister was about to utter an elaborate disclaimer, when I interposed, ' If you will help me to lay my hand upon the Nana I will give you a lakh of rupees.'

" The priest started as though electrified. I had appealed to his ruling passion, and he was evidently experiencing a tremendous mental struggle.

"'But the sin,' he pleaded, 'the inexpiable sin; you will hang him. It will be owing to my help, and he is very holy.'

"'True,' I answered; 'but then a lakh of rupees will enable you to purge yourself of a far greater enormity than the seizure of a rebel and murderer. See, I will add to the gift complete indemnity for all offences that you may have committed up to the present moment.'

"This turned the trembling scale. The old Twister sat for a moment nervously cracking his fingers, then he said :—'I will lead you to Nana Punt, but we must start at once, for he is moving northward. Ah! Govinda! who is that?'

"I turned, and caught sight of a dusky figure hurrying away from the door. I immediately despatched my orderly in pursuit, but the fleeting shadow had vanished in the mist.

" Before the sun was well above the horizon we were on our way. I was disguised as a native cavalry trooper, my face and hands being stained with a vegetable juice, and my apparel carefully selected by the Brahmin. I was well mounted, but my companion, who was soft and portly, travelled in a palanquin; our progress, therefore, was so slow that by nightfall we had done barely twenty miles, and were still three leagues short of the Nana's hiding-place. The bearers being dead-beat, refused to proceed until they had eaten and rested, and as the priest could neither walk nor ride, I proposed to proceed alone ; but Burabalang represented that without a certain pass-word, which he would not divulge to me, I should not be able to obtain entrance to the retreat. I had therefore to wait, kicking my heels till past midnight, when the Twister's team consented to go on. It was not till the sun was rising that we found ourselves outside the courtyard of a lonely *mutt*, or monastery, at the edge of a thick jungle. A small window in the massive gate was cautiously unbarred, and in reply to a whispered question from within, my companion muttered what sounded like ' *Hari Bôl*,' upon which the gate swung open. Burabalang explained that he was the Nana's domestic guru, and that I was a Bithoor sepoy flying from the English ; whereupon the people of the *mutt* received us cordially and gave us wheaten cakes and curd. They told us that the Nana, having suddenly received intimation of approaching danger from Cawnpore, had, accompanied by a few followers, ridden off shortly after midnight, his point being a small monastery in the heart of the jungle, some five-and-twenty miles away. When the palki-bearers learnt that we were about to penetrate the gloomy forest before them,

they fairly struck ; and neither the fear of punish-
ment nor the hope of reward would induce them
to trot another foot. Seeing this deadlock, I told
the Brahmin he must ride, and purchasing a stout
country cob, with a comfortable saddle, from one
of the lay brothers, I made my fat friend mount
and accompany me.   When we arrived at the
jungle monastery Burabalang was nearly dead with
fatigue, and could hardly gasp out his ' *Hari Bôl.*'
Here again we were late by some hours, and the
Nana had once more escaped us.   The porter, however, put us upon his track, and after a brief halt
we resumed the pursuit.   At the next resting-place
the bird had only just flown, and if our horses had
been able to do a mile gallop we should have
caught him ; but the animals were now suffering
from want of food, and it was impossible to get
them beyond the monastery gates.   Here, then, we
had to halt twelve hours to enable our cattle to
pull themselves together.   The Twister declared he
was a mass of aches and pains, that his head was
hot and his feet were cold, that he had a swelling
in his heart, and hot coals in his spine, and it
required all my energy and determination to prevent
his returning to Cawnpore.

" The course of the flight now took a north-
easterly direction ; the halting-places were some-

times temples, sometimes *mutts*, and occasionally the private residences of Brahmins; thus we journeyed on for a fortnight, always from twelve to twenty-four hours behind the fugitives. In this manner we crossed Oude, forded the Gunduck river and entered the Terai. It was now clear to me that the Nana was heading for the hills beyond Siliguri, in which wild country I feared he would give us the slip. Continuing to pass ourselves off as his followers, which in one sense we certainly were, we had no difficulty in getting supplies; our horses now held out well, and Burabalang was growing as hard as a dervish. Halting for the night near Kurseong we fell in with a shikari, who told us that our friends in advance were encamped within half a mile of us. Dead-beat though we were we pushed on and came upon the Nana's camp-fire, which he could not have left much more than an hour before. Here we found one of his followers dying from exhaustion. He recognized Burabalang and spoke to him without reserve. He told us that the Nana was now accompanied by only two attendants; five had died from fever, two had run away, and one had fallen victim to a snake. The Nana's original intention had been to reach the Khylasa Mountain, but hearing that the hill-people were murdering all the low-country

o

strangers that came in their way, he had turned towards Darjeeling with the intention of seeking an asylum at Lhassa. His sufferings had been excruciating, and he kept up his strength only by drenching himself with opium. The party, when they left the Ganges, had been mounted on Mahratta ponies of the rarest breed, and this accounted for the way in which they had kept ahead of us. We halted by the fire for some hours, for our limbs were so stiff with the cold that we were quite unable to sit on our horses. Long ere the dawn, the Nana's retainer died, not, however, before he had told us that warning of my intended pursuit had been conveyed to the Nana by a man whom I was employing in Cawnpore in a confidential capacity, and who had overheard my morning's conversation with the priest. Shortly after sunrise we resumed our march, but our progress was very slow, for the road was bad and we had no guide. We rode through Darjeeling at midnight. Burabalang implored me to stop for food and rest, but I was afraid the Nana would slip on through Sikkim, and it might take us years to run him down on the boundless plains of Thibet. A little way out of the town we came upon a dead pony, and about a mile further on we saw another, from which we knew that at any rate two of the fugitives were reduced to Shanks's mare. At daylight I saw for the first time the magnificent spectacle of the Snowy Range. Away to the left was Everest, with its helmet-like top, and in front of me was Kinchinjunga, gleaming like a king in silver armour enthroned among his barons. That morning we halted at a Buddhist temple, and here I noted a change in the pass-word. '*Hari Bôl*' no longer served; the countersign now was '*O màni pé mi hûn*,' and the Twister declared that these words would admit us into any monastery from Senchal to Lhassa. The room that we occupied had been vacated by the Nana that morning at sunrise, and in the stable, lying at its last gasp, was the pony that had carried the rebel leader from Bithoor.

"After a few hours' rest we again pressed forward, and snow having fallen during the previous night we could now track the fugitives by their foot-marks. Burabalang at once recognized and pointed out a short, broad indentation as the foot-print of the rebel chief. Shortly afterwards we learnt from some travelling Bhutia traders that three low-countrymen were struggling on about a mile ahead of us. We spurred forward, anticipating an early end to our tedious chase, when we suddenly found ourselves brought up by a deep and rapid river, once spanned by a cane bridge ; but the canes now floated uselessly in the stream, the Nana and his followers having secured a respite by cutting the suspending withies. Darkness was now coming on, and it was necessary for us to seek refuge for the night in a Lepcha's hut, and to wait till daylight for our host to conduct us to a ford. This threw us back twelve hours, but we clung to the track like sleuth-hounds. At noon that day our horses gave out and we, like our quarry, had to proceed on foot; my companion suffered a good deal from the cold, but I kept up his spirits by talking of the lakh of rupees that he was to receive and by enlarging on the pleasures and honours in store for him. At last we reached the foot of the Snowy Range, and here the divergent footprints told us that the party had separated. Two had strayed away to the west towards Nepaul, while the third had pressed on steadily up the slopes of Kinchinjunga. The marks that formed this trail were short and broad. The priest was in favour of leaving this track, which he pointed out led to certain death, and urged me to follow up the pair. I acquiesced, for I was certain that the man in front of us could not escape, and I wished to make sure of the identity of the others; they were not far off, and their progress was evidently slow and difficult. Every now and then we came upon an impression on the snow showing where one had stumbled and fallen, or had thrown himself down for a moment's rest. About noon we came upon both the fugitives ; one was lying on his back, the other on his side, and Burabalang at once recognized them as palace servants of Bithoor. The elder of the two was already dead ; the younger one, who was dying fast, in reply to our question as to the whereabouts of the Nana, pointed faintly towards Kinchinjunga, and then, exhausted by the effort, fell back and followed his companion to the abode of Yama. Quickly retracing our footsteps, we regained the Nana's trail just as the sun was setting. As the night came on, the cold became severe, and it was with intense satisfaction that I observed a light gleaming a little ahead of us; it was from a fire in front of the tent of a Thibetan pedlar, who readily gave us food and shelter for the night. At dawn I roused my companion and compelled him, though he pointed dolefully to his swollen feet, to rise and accompany me. He slowly trudged after me in sullen silence, and we had not ascended more than two miles when he sat down and refused by all the gods of his Pantheon to budge another inch. Testily bidding him return to the tent, I pressed

on, and with those short, broad footsteps in front
of me, I promised myself that in the course of
a few hours I should have captured the most
ruthless savage of the age. With no refreshment
save a few handfuls of snow, for I had to husband
my provisions, I continued clambering till sun-
down, then wrapping myself in a *poshtin* that I
had bought in the last monastery, I crept into a
cave that had probably once been the lair of a
wild beast. Here I ate a chupatti and drank a
little brandy; I intended to have a smoke, but
before I had lit my pipe I had fallen asleep.
The next day the sun and I were up together, and
Excelsior was still the word, but the snow being
deep and the gradient severe, nightfall found me
still at a considerable distance from the summit.
That night there was no cave for me, so I lay out in
the open. It was bitterly cold, but I managed to
snatch a few hours'. sleep, resuming my upward
march on the third day as fresh as a daisy.

"I still had a handful of dried peas and a
chupatti in my trousers' pocket, and this with a
few drops of brandy remaining in my flask furnished my breakfast. At eleven o'clock I was
within hail of the top, and by noon, sir, I stood
upon the summit. The stillness of these Hima-
layan solitudes, the intense loneliness of the eternal

snows, the pervading sense of immutability, filled
me with the most solemn sensations, but as I looked
wonderingly around me I started with joy; for,
seated not forty yards from where I stood was *a
man;* his arms were clasped around his knees, and
his head was leaning forward with the face turned
upwards towards the sky. A second glance,
however, convinced me that I was gazing upon a
corpse; the eyes were staring stonily, the mouth
was drawn back with a sort of scornful grin, and a
few light snowflakes that rested upon the livid flesh
remained unmelted. The face was that of a
Mahratta Brahmin, the holy mark was on the
forehead, the Peishwa's signet-ring was on the
finger; the form before me was the Nana! Yes—
within reach of my good right arm crouched the
bloody butcher of Bithoor. Overpowered by my
emotions, I drew my sabre and cut down with all
my strength upon his neck. The blade shivered in
a dozen pieces, but made no impression upon the
body, which was frozen to the temper of adamant.
I might as well have tried to cleave the Pillar of
Asoka. The sound of the blow rang across those
silent wastes, echoing from peak to peak like a
voice from another world. As it died away in the
far distance, an avalanche fell into an ice-bound
valley, and an eagle, startled from his eyry, floated

majestically to a distant crag.   But snow was falling, and it was past noon, so, forcing the signet-
ring from the finger of the frozen figure, I lost no
time in commencing the descent.   It had taken
me three days to get up, but I did the return
journey in six hours.   Near where I had left
Burabalang I stumbled over, and nearly fell upon,
what seemed to me to be a boulder of ice, but
which a closer inspection proved to be the unfortunate old Twister.   The Brahmin, deprived of
my stimulating presence, had allowed himself to
sink upon a snow-drift, where he rapidly froze
to death.

"My journey back was devoid of interest.   I
hastened by forced marches to Cawnpore, where I
delivered the ring to Neill, and explained how I
had accomplished my mission without spending a
cowrie of the lakh of rupees which he had promised to allot me.   Neill lost no time in reporting
the result of my expedition to Havelock, and each
expressed himself to be perfectly satisfied with the
zealous manner in which I had hunted the Nana
to his death.   But Havelock, always sensitive regarding the reputation of his subordinates, hesitated to publish the story to the world.   It was so
unprecedented, so full of marvel, so utterly incredible to those who did not know me, that he

feared it would evoke a storm of derision. You
see I had no further evidence to support my tale
than the ring and the frozen body on the peak, by
this time probably buried in the drifting snow. I
had not been able to report myself to the authorities during the pursuit, and I had neglected to
do so in the course of my return. My sole witness,
the Brahmin priest, was dead, ' and Bowlong's fair
fame,' observed the good General, ' must not be
lightly exposed to the aspersions of malice and the
attacks of ignorance.' I acquiesced for the time,
but was determined as soon as the campaign was
over to compel both Havelock and Neill to see that
justice was done me, but, as ill luck would have it,
within three months of my return to Cawnpore
their earthly career had terminated, and, for the
sake of the unimpeached veracity that is my
dearest treasure, I have preserved unbroken silence
till to-night. Some sort of version of the affair,
however, curiously enough, did get abroad, and for
a time it was believed that I had followed the Nana
to the top of *Everest!* and had there pelted him
to death with snow-balls. This, Sir Mundus, I
need not tell you, was palpably absurd, for no
living man has ever yet set foot on the summit of
the highest mountain in the world."

Sir Mundus, taking from his pocket a large

note-book and a little pencil, now rose, and, grasping our Chief's hand, said, in a voice of deep emotion :—" Colonel Bowlong, this feat of yours shall no longer be hidden in the gloom of official neglect. You, sir, shall emerge from the unmerited obscurity in which you have for so long a period languished. I will, with your assistance, now proceed to note down the heads of your incomparable exploit, and when I return to England I will, from my place in Parliament, proclaim the matchless fortitude, constancy, and endurance with which you, almost singlehanded, hunted down the Tiger of Cawnpore. I will compel the British Government to recognize your unexampled achievement, or I will make the country ring and sparkle with your wrongs. I will——"

The Colonel, who had made several attempts to introduce a word, now broke in upon the legislator's eloquence. " No, no, Sir Mundus, your kindness is unspeakable, and no doubt your influence is very great, but I can't have my name dragged into the House of Commons. The time that has passed, my extreme disinclination to publicity, my—my sensitive regard for my character as a truth-telling man——"

Here Sir Mundus eagerly interposed :—" Your brilliant action shall not continue to be hidden. I will not hear of it, sir; you modest heroes are just the men that we Radicals must fight for; the blatant swashbuckler with the House of Lords behind him can take care of himself, but silent, retiring merit needs a mouthpiece, and, Colonel Bowlong, you shall find that mouthpiece in Mundus Trotter. From my place in Parliament I will publish your achievement to the nation, and will vindicate your claims."

The Colonel held up his hand imploringly. "My achievement was the merest trifle, and claims I have absolutely none."

Sir Mundus, silencing the old gentleman with a dramatic wave of the arm, continued :—"The Secretary of State for India shall have no rest until he has caused every record-office in the land to be ransacked for evidence of your services. You shall be made a C.B., Colonel Bowlong, perhaps a K.C.B. From my place in——"

The Colonel, who now disclosed symptoms of serious agitation, here placed both his hands upon the statesman's narrow shoulders. "Sir Mundus Trotter, I beg you to listen to me. If you will not have mercy upon my modesty, at least respect the sanctity of the mess-table. True, we are now in the verandah, yet you are still my guest, and I have unveiled to you this secret of the

eternal snows in the assured confidence that the
mystery would never be made the subject of
public comment. I appeal to you not to give us
occasion to complain that Eastern hospitality was
betrayed by Western ingratitude. Spare us the
necessity and yourself the shame of such a sad
reproach." And the old man removed one of his
hands in order to mop his heated face with a large
bandana.

"Nay, sir, if you urge your protest on those
grounds, of course I yield," said the M.P., evidently
speaking with strong reluctance. "I yield, but,
believe me, this morbid self-depreciation does you
and yours very grievous harm ; you should be at
this moment a General Officer, and Aide-de-Camp
to the Queen. Think of it, my dear sir, and if
before I leave India I receive your permission to do
so, I will from my place in Parliament——."

"Enough, sir," smiled the Colonel with a sigh of
exquisite relief; "enough, I have your promise.
Now we will close the evening with a bowl of
Pandour punch. Did you ever taste 'Samson with
his hair on,' Sir Mundus? No? Bless my soul!
Here, mess-boy, quick, bring brandy and curaçoa,
three green chillies, and a box of matches." The
composition was soon prepared, and Colonel Bowlong's solicitude for his guest was such that when

the politician was taken home in his host's carriage at midnight, although he still referred with much emphasis to his contemplated exertions on behalf of his friend from "plashinparlmnt," the orator was in no condition to exert material influence upon a debate, and when he awoke the next morning his mind, in so far as the events of the previous night were concerned, was as colourless as the snows that shrouded the Colonel's secret.

DIDONE;

OR,

THE COLONEL'S LOVE TALE.

——o——

ONE evening we were discussing a wedding that
had lately taken place in the station, a union that
local gossip ascribed more to the enterprise of the
lady than to the advances of the gentleman.

"I can't believe," observed the Major, as he
gravely scanned the rowel of his left spur, "that
a woman ever went so far as actually, don't you
know, to propose to a fellow."

"Don't be too certain of that," chirruped the
junior Cornet, shaking his curly little head
sapiently, "I can tell you I've known some deucéd
curious things happen over *that* line of country."

Colonel Bowlong regarded the lad approvingly.
"Snapper is right," said he. "Why, I myself
was proposed to in the most determined manner
when I was a young fellow, and by a very beautiful
young woman too. By George! it required the

help of an entire British Army Corps to enable me to escape her."

"Was that in Europe or in India, Colonel?" inquired Snapper, in a confidential tone, as though he and his chief were co-proficients in mysteries from which the rest of us were excluded.

"The event took place in Africa," said the Colonel, not so much replying to the Cornet as addressing us all, and the circumstances are so remarkable that I think they will bear repetition.

The speaker called for a whiskey-and-soda; whereupon we closed round his long arm-chair, and the tale began :—

"In the beginning of '68 I exchanged into a Regiment stationed at Aden, and before I had joined it a month, I was, for my sins, sent on detachment to Perim. Here I found myself shelved for six of the hottest months in the year, with nothing to amuse me but a few books and an old telescope. I stood it for over a fortnight and then began to think of suicide, but while I was debating as to the least objectionable method of making my quietus, a Suez buggalow touched at Perim on her way to Massowah. My mind was at once made up, and tossing all thoughts of self-destruction to the winds, I handed over charge of the Island to the sergeant, and, boarding the buggalow, sailed to Abyssinia, intending to spend the remainder of my time in shooting elephants and guinea-fowls.

"Find me out! who was to do that? In those days the Island was never inspected more than once in five years. Have you never heard of the sportsman who did his tour of Perim in Pall Mall?

"On board the buggalow I made friends with an old Coptic priest who was on his way to visit the *Abuna* or Metropolitan at Magdala. The priest easily persuaded me to accompany him as far as the Tigré country, where he assured me I should find plenty of game, and should receive hospitable treatment from the inhabitants. We landed at Arkiko, near Massowah, and there I purchased a fine dromedary of the kind known among the Arabs as wind-racers, or rapid-goers, but as my companion's mount was only a feeble old donkey I had no opportunity of putting my animal's speed and endurance to the proof; later on, however, as I shall show you, he might have stood me in right good stead. After a short but very interesting journey, we arrived at Axum, and were warmly welcomed by a Coptic deacon, Paul Erasmus by name, who, in former years, had been a fellow-student of the priest's at Cairo, and was now domiciled in Abyssinia. The deacon told us that, as it was custom-

ary to present all strangers of respectability to the
Princess Regnant, he would arrange for our reception by Her Majesty upon the following day, after
which the priest would be at liberty to continue
his journey to Galla-land, and I should most
probably obtain permission to shoot in the royal
preserves either at Axum or at Adowa.

"On the day appointed for the interview, the
priest arrayed himself in his clerical vestments,
and I put on my full-dress tunic, which, in view
of the possibility of introductions at Native Courts,
I had rammed into my valise before leaving
Perim. It was a beautiful day, cold but with a
bright sun, and the whole town was *en fête* for the
Negus's birthday. At noon we heard a great
blowing of conches and firing of guns, which, we
were told, announced that the Princess had taken
her seat upon the throne, and in the course of a
few minutes a grand functionary of State, a sort
of Lord Chamberlain, dressed in a lion's skin and
three ostrich-feathers, came, accompanied by a
score or two of spearmen, to inform us that the
Far-Shining Didoné, Queen of Adowa, Princess of
Axum, and heiress-presumptive of Lijkasa, King
of kings, Emperor of Ethiopia, and Negus of
Abyssinia, had commanded him, Limpopo, her
poor slave and herald, to communicate to us the

P

fact that her pellucid Majesty had graciously consented to concede to us the privilege of crawling to the steps of her throne."

The Colonel here paused for a drink, and then continued :—

" This language, however, was purely figurative, for, in point of fact, we walked into the hall on our hind legs like Christians, and were ceremoniously escorted by Limpopo to the royal daïs, where we were given a seat upon a stuffed giraffe ; the skin was well tanned and, being filled with silk-cotton, somewhat resembled the *pouffe* of a modern drawing-room. The following conversation then took place, the designation applied to us having reference to the colour of our apparel. The Princess began :—

" ' Wherefore hath the ugly old black man come? '

" ' To pray, your Serenity,' replied Limpopo, who before admitting us to the presence had subjected us to a severe cross-examination through the medium of an interpreter.

" ' And the comely red youth ? '

" ' To slay, O Diaphaneity.'

" ' Where the praying ? '

" ' In Magdala, Lady of Light.'

" ' And the slaughter ? '

" ' Here, if thy Brilliancy permitteth it.'

" ' Doth the red youth slay warriors ? '

" ' Nay, Sunbeam, men he slayeth not, but the elephant, the zebra, the giraffe, the hyena, the quagga, and the double-horned rhinoceros he moweth down like autumn rushes.'

" ' Hath he the heart to meet a lion ? '

" ' His heart containeth the courage of seven lions, bright Star of the Morning.'

" ' Give unto each of them salt. The ugly old black man may proceed upon his journey, the comely red youth will tarry here.'

" During this curious scene the Princess twice removed her veil and disclosed a face not unlike that of a Circassian ; she seemed to be about four-and-twenty years old, and, so far as I could discover, was of a tall and graceful figure. On the little finger of her right hand she wore an enormous gold ring, in which was a fine turquoise surrounded by rubies and emeralds ; this, I afterwards learnt, was peculiarly an emblem of Tigrani royalty, in fact, the ring alone constituted the Axum regalia, neither crown nor sceptre being known to the Abyssinians.

" On the day after our presentation, my Coptic friend started for Magdala; and I received a courteously worded invitation, through Limpopo and the interpreter, to occupy a small house

P 2

situated within the precincts of the home-park.
The tenement was provided with such simple
articles of furniture as a single man might
require—a heap of otter-skins formed my bed,
three stuffed quagga-hides did duty for seats, while
some pots and pans and a low wooden table
enabled me occasionally to display the skill of my
old negress-cook in a modest entertainment to
Paul Erasmus the deacon. There was a stall close
by for my dromedary, and not far off stood a
kennel full of hounds, which I was informed were
at my disposal. I was furnished with horses from
the Queen's stables, and had at my service the
royal huntsmen and a host of attendants. One
thing alone was forbidden to me, and that was to
pay for anything. Nobody was allowed to receive
money from me : whatever I wanted was at once
supplied free, gratis, and for nothing. In a word, I
was in clover, and so far as sport went, I made the
most of my unrivalled opportunities. I was in
the saddle every morning before daylight, and
spent the entire day either in the woods or on the
mountains, never returning to my cottage until
the sun had set and it was too dark to shoot. And
the bags that I made ! The interpreter's reply to
the Queen was very nearly literally correct, for I
secured specimens of all the animals he had

mentioned and of many more. The forests teemed with big game, and although I sent all my finest trophies to the palace and distributed an immense number among the huntsmen, my stock of heads and skins soon became so large that I despaired of ever conveying a tenth part of them to the coast. In the end I thought myself superlatively lucky to be able to carry merely my own head and skin there. But I could not anticipate what was coming, and my happiness was complete. In this way a month passed like a flash. I had forgotten Aden, Perim, parades, officer of the day, courts-martial, and all the round of duties of the military mill as though I had never laboured at it. As for the Princess, she stood to me in the light of a good fairy who supplied my wants before they were expressed; but I neither saw her nor heard of her until one morning, when emerging from my hunting-lodge equipped for a quagga-hunt, I observed the Queen mounted on a fine white Sanga ox that carried a pair of horns quite eight feet in span. Her Majesty was followed by a phalanx of mounted spearmen with wild horses' tails floating from the heads of their lances. The party was making its way across the park in the direction of the cottage, and very picturesque it looked looming through the white mist. On her arrival, the Queen told me, through an interpreter, that she had come to join in the chase that day, and when she heard that we were going to a part of her preserves known as the five ravines, she expressed her confidence that we should enjoy good sport.

" Her desire, of course, was law, and although I was selfish enough to wish Her Majesty at Jericho, I declared myself overwhelmed by her condescension and enchanted at the prospect of her company. The trumpeters performed a flourish, the hounds bayed in answer, the spearmen waved their lances, and off we went, the Sanga ox leading the way. We had a great day with the quags : I killed nine or ten, and the Queen, who was a capital shot, accounted for five. She was radiant with triumph, and on her way home announced her intention of coming out with me again, and sure enough she and her Sanga turned up true to time the next morning, and so it went on until our going afield together became an established custom.

" I had now begun to understand the language, and could manage to keep up a desultory conversation with Her Majesty on passing incidents. She was always ready to talk, and I soon formed a most favourable opinion of her good sense and

amiability. At that time I never dreamt of anything like love rising between us—I regarded her,
in fact, as a right good fellow and a capital shooting companion. Ah! I little knew what volcanic
elements lay beneath that smiling surface.

" One day a circumstance occurred which, if I had
read its significance aright, would have served as a
warning to me of rocks ahead. We were engaged
in a lion-hunt. The Queen and I had distanced all
the huntsmen, and when the lion turned at bay,
we were alone with the dogs. Seeing that the
royal beast was much confused by the determined
onslaught of some twelve couple of sturdy boar-
hounds, the huntress leaped from her ox and
gallantly charged the quarry with her light spear.
The weapon entered the animal's side and broke
off short, whereupon the maddened brute, shaking
himself clear of the dogs, sprang upon his new
assailant, struck her to the ground, and stood
roaring over her. I had a heavy rifle with me, and,
firing from the distance of four and a half paces,
it was no great feat for me to drive a bullet into
the lion's brain. I assisted the Queen to rise, and
found that she had been struck by the creature's
chest, but had escaped its claws, and though
considerably shaken and momentarily quite un-
nerved, she, wonderful to narrate, was uninjured,

As I raised her from the ground she lay for a moment in my arms, her great black gazelle-like eyes regarding me tenderly. It was an impressive scene, gentlemen : in the foreground lay the dead lion, surrounded by the exhausted hounds ; in the background stretched an expanse of grey rock-broken waste, with not even a mimosa to challenge its sterility ; and in the centre was I, a not unpicturesquely-clad hunter, supporting the half-fainting form of the lovely Princess of Tigré."

"Believes every word he's saying," whispered the Doctor to me ; "never witnessed such complete self-delusion in my life."

The narrator went on :—

"For a brief space she lay reposing in my arms like a languorous odalisque. She soon pulled herself together though, and, holding out her hand, gave me the royal ring, which I placed respectfully upon my little finger. In another minute she was in the saddle, once more a vigorous young Diana, loudly sounding her jewelled conch in summons of her train.

"That evening Limpopo came to my dwelling and peremptorily demanded the ring, explaining that I was allowed to wear it only till sunset, and that it was an unprecedented mark of honour that it had been given to me at all; but I refused to surrender the jewel without an order from Her Majesty, and the herald had to go back empty-handed. Later on he returned with the required command. It was written in Amharic and ran thus: ' *Give back the ring, O beloved of Didoné, for it is not hers but the State's.*' That loan of the ring had a deep significance: it showed me to be a highly-favoured person, and thenceforward Limpopo became my enemy.

" On that day week I received an invitation to dine at the palace. It was the first time I had been thus honoured, and it was clearly a sequence of the lion-hunt. Donning my red tunic, I repaired at eight o'clock to the royal domicile. Passing through the outer court, the entrance-hall, and the audience-chamber, I was led through many a devious corridor to the royal apartments, and a heavy curtain of tiger-skins being lifted, I found myself face to face with the Queen. Didoné, attired in purple and cloth of gold, lay, gracefully reclining, upon a heap of wild-swan skins; she was attended by a single slave, a tall Nubian woman, who, standing motionless with folded arms behind her royal mistress, resembled a magnificent ebony caryatid. The room was lighted by silver lamps suspended from the ceiling, and was perfumed with the delicate aroma of the diamond-rose, the petals of which were strewn upon the floor.

"Our dinner was served upon a large gold tray, placed upon the carpet, and though seated *à la Turque*, I made myself as comfortable as the situation allowed. On the whole I dined fairly well, washing down gilded quails and scented apples with large draughts of a violet-coloured wine, in flavour resembling Chablis. During the repast the royal band sent forth from a distant chamber a not unpleasing medley of conches and kettle-drums, which was not loud enough to disturb our conversation. After dinner, pipes and coffee were introduced. Didoné did not smoke, but in order that I might not be without companionship, she commanded the Nubian to seat herself at a respectful distance and to afford me moral support by consuming the contents of a narghilé.

"The smoking over, my royal hostess arose and led me through a long range of rooms filled with curiosities in the shape of hunting trophies, and specimens of various forms of barbaric art. These having been leisurely examined and admired, she conducted me to an apartment that I concluded was her boudoir. It was more like a large jewel-case than a room. The roof was delicately arabesqued in blue and silver, and was supported upon graceful columns of an antique Moorish pattern. These columns, which were plated with silver, coruscated with every motion of the observer, for they were studded with precious stones. The walls were hung with a rich tapestry of a deep terra-cotta hue, relieved here and there by the boss of a flower woven in with silver wire. Upon a small enamelled table lay a highly-ornamented dagger, slim and shapely as its owner, and by its side was a round gold box. In the centre of the room a tiny fountain splashed into a marble basin, dashing its sparkling spray against the blossom of a *tromo*, or giant serpent-flower, that diffused dreamy fragrance from a silver jar.

"On the floor of an alcove were spread costly rugs and cushions from Khartoum; by their side glowed the skin of the lion that I had shot seven days before, and a large lamp of curiously wrought iron swinging from the roof, withheld rather than diffused the rays of the perfumed flame within.

"Sinking gracefully upon the lion's skin, Didoné motioned to me to be seated by her side, and taking up a dulcimer that lay near her, she sang me a plaintive little Tigrani ballad which, translated, runs something like this :—

" ' Youth, dominion, treasure, health,
      All, all are mine ;
    Yet amidst this godlike wealth,
        Yes, yes, I pine ;
    That for which my nature yearns,
    That to which my hope returns,
    That for which my soul's heart burns
        Canst thou divine ? "

" ' Youth is but a fever-dream,
    Empire but a marish gleam,
    Beauty but a cynic's theme,
        One boon denied ;
    Shall I breathe the secret ?—nay,
        Spare, spare my pride,
    Thou canst guess what I would say,
        Yet, yet must hide.'

" There was a wild melody in the simple lay that perfectly enchanted me, while the strain of melancholy infused into the words by the singer, and the pathetic sadness of her face as she wailed forth the concluding line, with her earnest almost beseeching eyes fixed upon mine, went straight to my heart.

" The song was followed by a long silence which neither of us seemed inclined to break, and the only sound that for some minutes disturbed the stillness was the splash of the little fountain. As I sat enraptured by the music, glamoured by the romantic surroundings, and growing every moment more and more fascinated by the superb loveliness of the Queen, the wilful beauty suddenly stretched a shapely arm towards me, and with a bewitching smile pressed the royal ring upon my mouth. My ears were still ringing with the tender notes of the dulcimer, my brain was throbbing wildly with the strange significance of the ballad, and my blood was coursing madly through my veins from the effect of the violet wine. The heavy perfume of the snake-flower, coupled with the intoxicating fumes rising from a censer that the night wind was slowly swinging to and fro, served to deprive me of what little self-control and sense of decorum still remained to me, and I stretched out my arms to my bewitching hostess, whose glorious eyes beamed upon me with so ravishing a radiance and——I was immediately floored by a blow from the fist of the Amazon in waiting, whose presence I had entirely forgotten. After this I remember no more. I awoke the next morning in my own cottage with a racking headache and a confused vision of silver lamps, snake-flowers, and eyes such as those which of old lured the beholder into the realm of the Lorelei and the Mist-maiden.

"'That confounded blue wine,' I groaned, 'catch me drinking any more of it!'

"That day I shot badly, and was very nearly expended by a rhinoceros which killed my horse and mortally wounded one of the huntsmen ; and in the course of the evening I received a strip of vellum on which was written,—

"'*Pata, pata ai nireewis, ma ku flior, Dalitti kosina.*' 'Take care, take care, O cherished one. To her that shinest thou art very dear.'

"After this I ought to have packed up and marched, but fool-like I lingered. In truth, I began to find a difficulty in detaching myself from Axum ; this Ethiopian girl was gradually exercising a mysterious influence over my volition, an influence of which I felt the growth, but was unable to resist the attraction. At first I fought hard against the power that was enslaving me, but after a time I ceased to struggle, and before that week was over I was as firmly fixed to Axum as a tree in the royal park. In a short time came the crisis.

"We had gone out as usual for a hunt, when the Queen, saying that she would not shoot that day, suddenly dismissed our attendants and proposed a quiet ride in the shade of the forest. The day was intensely hot, and the increasing sultriness indicated the approach of a storm. Conversing gaily upon various subjects, Didoné led me deeper and deeper into the wilderness. Giant creepers obstructed our path, tangled undergrowth and treacherous swamps added to the difficulty of the way, and all the time the low rumbling of distant thunder warned us, though in vain, that prudence counselled our turning home. When I thought we were inextricably entrapped in a wild-looking spot, half moss, half bush, in the very heart of the forest, Didoné pointed to a tongue of firm soil that led to a sort of oasis of slightly higher ground, thickly embosomed in large black trees of the densest foliage. From the centre of this insulated grove jutted a massive rock, the dark and gloomy appearance of which was well in keeping with the sombre aspect of the surrounding scenery. Every moment the sky became more obscure, and the stillness of the forest grew more intense: not a leaf rustled, not a bird twittered, not an insect stirred. Didoné dismounted and, signing to me to follow, began, lance in hand, to part the thick rushes that grew round the base of the rock. These I soon perceived concealed the entrance to a cavern. My companion entered cautiously, as though afraid of disturbing some wild beast; and as I followed her, I regretted that I had given my arms to one of our attendants whom we had dismissed an hour before. The den was silent as the grave, pitch-dark, and heavy with mephitic vapours.

" ' Father, it is Didoné,' said the Queen, addressing some one who was invisible to me.

" ' Welcome ! ' replied a tremulous voice from the
recesses of the cave.

" ' It is dark, father.'

" In a moment the red flame of a torch flared
forth and disclosed a man, bent with age and
emaciated by suffering, whose long white hair fell
in tangled masses upon his skeleton shoulders, and
whose cavernous eyes shone with an unnatural
brilliancy that told of a disordered intellect. With
one hand he held up the newly-lighted torch, and
with the other he steadied his tottering frame by
grasping a projecting fragment of rock. The hermit
evidently knew Didoné well, for he expressed no
surprise at her visit, and after one piercing glance
at me, he for a time ignored my presence.

" ' What seeks my royal daughter of the sun ? '

" ' How are the stars, father ? '

" ' Bland as thy mother's eyes.'

" ' Doth the spark, thou callest mine, bid fair ? '

" ' Thy planet, daughter, gloweth like fine gold.'

" Didoné paused for a moment and then in a low
voice continued :—

" ' When Tagazze had doomed thee for a wizard
to the flame, whose was the hand that unbound
thee at the stake ? '

" ' Thine, kindly orb, 'twas thine,' quavered the recluse.

" ' Dost recall what thou didst swear to me as thy chains fell among the smoking faggots ? '

" The old man bent his head in silence.

" ' Speak, father, if three short years have not dimmed thy memory.'

" There was no reply, and the Queen stamped her foot petulantly. The hermit stood bowed before her, the wind moaned through the cave, and as it fanned the torch I could perceive that the old man's eyes were fixed on vacancy, and that his lips were moving as though in communion with some invisible presence, but no word escaped him in response to Didoné's question.

" ' Must I tell thee then, O perjured one, O wretch whose word is as the fleeting brook ? Thou didst swear, O Guldu, by the heart of Prester John, yea, by the mighty Priest-King's heart thou didst swear it, to do my hest through earth, through air, through fire, through water.'

" The old man replied hoarsely,—

" ' 'Twas even so, O daughter of the day.'

" ' Father, thou shalt obey my bidding now,' she said.

" ' Let the child of the dawn command, and

Q

though she demand my life, yea, by the heart of
the dead Priest-King, Guldu will yield it.'

" For a brief space Didoné was silent, and then,
as though by a tremendous effort, she cried,—

" 'Bind us in the bond of blood at the point of
Prester's spear,' and as she spoke a loud roll of
thunder heralded the storm without.

" ' Thee and him?' inquired the hermit, trembling
violently, ' he is not as we are.'

" ' That is for *my* judgment—thou art not the
arbiter; thy word is passed, father, straightway bind
us twain.'

" The old man's eyes gleamed with a strange
brightness, his lips still moved, but no sound
escaped them.

" ' Thou art reading the future,' cried Didoné,
' while my concern is with the present. Leave thy
forecasting, comply with my behest and let me go.'

" ' Forbear, forbear!' wailed the seer, 'that path
leadeth to the flame that consumeth the heart.
Rather slay him with a poisoned kiss than be
coupled to him by the assegai. I hear thy sobs.
upon the midnight air, I see thy tears upon a
widowed couch ; there is still time to save thee
from thy sorrow '——

" ' Peace, peace! thy word is passed. Conjoin
us in the bond.'

" She spoke with so imperious and minatory an ·
air that the old man, overcome by her vehemence,
replied :—

" ' The soil that the death-flower loveth best is
the broken heart of a maiden ; come, stand before
me, thou and he.'

" And we stood side by side in front of the recluse.

" The torch lighted the rugged walls of the cavern
with lambent tongues of flame, which rose and fell
with the eddying wind, and as my eyes grew more
accustomed to the uncertain light, I perceived that
we were standing in front of an ancient sarcophagus. Kneeling before the tomb, the anchorite
spoke as follows :—

" ' A thousand years have passed away, O mighty
Prester John, since thou wert laid to rest ; and now
a daughter of thy royal line summons thee to her
bridal. May I disturb thy saintly slumbers ? Say,
royal Priest of Habesh, shall I roll back the guard-
ing stone and live ? '

" As he uttered the last word a faint blue light
played for a moment over the marble and disappeared.

" ' Ah ! he is benign, he is benign,' cried Didoné
triumphantly.

" The old man clasped his skinny hands together
and groaned :—

"'Aye, it is written in the book of doom; daughter, thy hest must speed,' and with an effort, which in one so frail surprised me, he pushed back the heavy slab of black marble that covered the sarcophagus. Within the tomb reposed a gigantic skeleton. A golden fillet crowned its head, a silver girdle encircled its waist, and an iron spear lay by its side. Raising the skeleton until it towered erect against the rocky wall, he carefully removed the girdle and bade each of us uncover our left arm. Then with the spear blade, which was as sharp as a razor, he lanced a small circle upon the middle of the inner part of the fore-arm of each of us, and carefully joining the two wounds, he bound our bleeding arms together with the girdle. Then raising the wrists of the skeleton, he for a moment enclosed our necks in its bony grip, and as he did so I seemed to feel the rigid clutch tighten on my throat. Then slowly disengaging the fleshless hands, he raised them aloft as though in the act of blessing, and in a hollow voice chanted the following words :—

"'Daughter, throb forth thy crimson pledge
　　Straight to thy loved one's heart,
　Son, pulsate back thy living gage,
　　Her pledge's counterpart.
　And one I bind as the winter wind
　　Is linked to the summer bloom,

But one is bound as the rock to ground,
And each must abide the doom.
For joined by the rush of the scarlet stream,
By the pang of the Prester's spear,
By the silver zone, by the grasp of bone,
By the flow of the coming tear,
Ye both are knit in the crimson thread
For bliss may it be—or pain.
Now seal the pact, for the rite is sped,
And the grave must close again.'

"Then the old man hissed in my ear :—

"'Nazarene, kiss thy bride.'

"Didoné inclined her face to mine, and as our lips met, the storm without burst forth in deafening diapasons. Amid the roaring of the wind and the crashing of the forest trees, the hermit's voice, acquiring strength with every word, arose in solemn accents :—

"'By Death and Eternity, by Eternity and Death, do I bind you. Death, and Death alone, shall sever you, but in Eternity ye shall re-unite ; by the spear of Prester, by the God Obi, by '—and here his voice sank into an inaudible whisper—'do I affiance you. Eternal is the bond, Eternal, ETERNAL, ETERNAL.'

"He ceased. The swelling thunder of the tempest sounded our marriage hymn, while, as the anchorite reverentially lowered the skeleton into the sepulchre, there seemed to arise from the depths of the marble, a mournful ' Amen ! '

"After letting us stand for a brief space where he had placed us, the old man released our arms, and devoutly restoring the girdle to the tomb, replaced the covering slab. Then, turning to us, he applied some styptic leaves to our lacerations, and, blowing the expiring torch into a flame, showed us the way to the mouth of the cavern.

"Hand in hand we issued forth, and mounting our animals rode on through the deepening storm. Didoné was wrapped in thought, and seemed to be deeply impressed either with the solemnity of the rite or with the old man's warning which she had so recklessly disregarded ; as for me, I was completely dazed and bewildered. We rode home without exchanging a word.

"After this awe-inspiring episode I felt, so to speak, as though I could not call my soul my own. The spirit of that weird rite had indeed entered my very blood, the skeleton's hand was never from my neck, Didoné's kiss was ever on my lips, that doleful ' Amen ' was always in my ear. If now and then under the influence of the morning air, or a sudden flush of youthful health, my spirit rose to thoughts of flight, I suddenly felt the constricting fold of the fleshless fingers upon my throat, and I heard the sacramental 'Eternal, eternal, eternal' echoing through the dreary chambers of my brain, while, like a never-failing refrain, came that voice from the grave sealing the ordinance with its sad 'Amen.'"

"I wonder if the tale is true," whispered the doctor to me, earnestly. "By Jove! I believe there's something more than hallucination here."

"On the day following this adventure," continued the Colonel, "I arose to go afield as usual, but found, to my surprise, neither animals nor attendants. In place of the dozen or so of huntsmen that ordinarily grouped themselves at daylight around my garden-gate, there stood Limpopo, stern and self-contained as usual. He brought a message from the Queen : 'Didoné, our Lady of Light, commandeth thee to remain within to-day. Hounds and horses must be rested. Thou thyself needest repose, so doth her Brilliancy.'

"These being the orders, I spent the morning in writing up my diary, and in cleaning my guns, after which I lay down with a book and my pipe on a heap of skins and soon fell asleep. About noon, however, I was aroused by a terrific blowing of conches and beating of calabash drums. I started to my feet and saw about a thousand armed men drawn up outside my dwelling. They were headed by Limpopo, wearing his herald's robes, lion's skin, ostrich feathers, and all the rest. He carried on his head a small packet wrapped in a white squirrel-skin, which, while he shot a malignant glance at me, he deposited with extreme ceremony in my right hand, saying :—

" ' This, O fortunate one, is from cur Lady of Light, Didoné the Queen, Didoné the Lovely, Didoné the Chaste. Receive—rejoice—accept.'

" He then waved his spear, and the armed host, discharging their muskets into the air, gave a yell that might have been heard at Massowah. Limpopo then placed himself at their head and led them back, with conches blowing and drums beating, in a stately march to the palace.

" On removing the outer covering of the packet, I found a sandal-wood box, within this was one of ivory, inside which was one of silver, which in its turn contained one of gold. This I opened with much curiosity and found therein—a cinder !

"Suspecting from the parade which accompanied the presentation of this apparently worthless article that it might symbolize something of importance, I stepped over to the house of the Coptic deacon, and, relating the episode, asked whether he could explain it and advise me how to act.

" ' That token is unmistakable,' he replied, adding with an air of extreme interest, ' but surely you have something more to tell me : the cinder represents an advanced stage of—friendship. If you seek advice, half-confidences are useless. Relate to me without reserve all that has passed, and I will to the best of my power advise you. One thing, at least, is clear : some sort of betrothal must have taken place between you. The cinder——but tell me the circumstances. The matter may be one of life or death.'

" Thus adjured, I told the Copt everything that had taken place from the day of the lion-hunt till the present hour. He smote his mouth with his palm and said :—

" ' I was sure of it—the cinder could mean but one thing. Didoné invites you to fulfil your troth by marrying her within the week, according to the Amharic ritual.'

" ' And how is one to reply to such an invitation ? ' I asked with a sinking heart, for I did not want to spend the remainder of my life buried away among the Abyssinian hills.

" ' That is easily done,' he answered, with a smile ; ' you send the lady a red rose.'

" ' What does that imply ? '

" ' Joyful compliance, of course.'

" ' Why " *of course?* " ' I inquired.

" ' No man in his senses would refuse the overtures of an Abyssinian Queen,' he answered, adding significantly, 'particularly after things have gone so far as they have with you and the Princess Regnant.'

" ' How does one convey a refusal ? ' I asked, desperately.

" ' A refusal is expressed by sending your admirer an old sandal, but it is a churlish action, and in this case would be fraught with extreme danger. Have a care what you do ; these people are demons when you cross them.'

" ' Is there not a less offensive way of escaping from the position ? '

" ' A black stone is equally effective, but,' he continued, earnestly, ' my dear sir, consider well before you venture upon such an unequivocal expression of contempt. You little know the character of the woman with whom you are dealing.'

" He continued for a time in the same strain, but the delicacy of the dilemma stimulated me. I shook off my torpor, and enclosing a black pebble in the gold box, packed it as I had received it, and that evening carried it myself to the palace.

" As I returned across the park in the gathering

gloom, I felt my torpor re-asserting itself; I seemed to hear the mournful utterance of the skeleton; its fingers were again tightening round my wind-pipe, and through the rustling of the branches came the words : 'Eternal—eternal—eternal is the bond!'

"On reaching the cottage I ought to have immediately saddled my dromedary and made tracks for the coast, but the re-action from the sudden spasm of energy that had animated me was complete. Every moment my inertia deepened, and by the time I entered the house I felt as though I were, for all purposes of manly volition, wrapped hand and foot in a ponderous shroud of lead.

"The next day when I opened my door for a draught of morning air, I was confronted by three of the royal spearmen, who instantly gave point at me. I banged the door in their faces and heard the three spear-heads pierce the wood. I ran for my revolver, but found, to my extreme astonishment, that all my weapons had been silently removed during the night. I then tried the back-door, but found it guarded as closely as the front. I opened a window, and narrowly escaped a vicious lunge at my neck by a grim warrior on guard there; in a word, the house was closely beleaguered by armed men. At night they lighted large fires and bivouacked under the trees, but still kept sentries on my doors and windows. My food, which hitherto had been of the best quality and oppressively abundant, now became bad and scanty. No one visited me, and the negress cook, who was allowed to enter the house once daily, was mute to all inquiries. Thus three days passed in miserable uncertainty, and I began to think that I had been a trifle too unceremonious in declining her Majesty's alliance. On the evening of the third day I heard the royal conches sounding, and I knew that I might expect soon to receive a communication from the Palace. Perhaps the Queen was about to repeat her gracious offer. The royal music drew near, the door was dashed open, and I saw Didoné herself, surrounded by a dozen stalwart Nubians bearing scimetars, that glittered in the torch-light and seemed as sharp as razors. The Queen was robed in leopard-skins; in one hand she carried the dagger that I had seen lying on the table of her boudoir, and in the other the round gold box that stood by its side. She seated herself on an ivory throne, brought by an attendant. Limpopo, in full war-paint, and grasping an enormous spear, stood on her right hand, and as he took up his position he regarded me with a triumphant stare of gratified malignity. As for Didoné, I never before saw her look so beautiful, but all trace of affection had vanished from her face, her large eyes flashed with anger, and her little hands played feverishly with the dagger.

" ' Graceless jerboa ! ' she began, addressing me, as I rose from my otter-skins.

" ' Thou leprous swine of the filthy black pit ! ' interposed Limpopo, speaking in a loud, harsh voice.

" ' Lady of Light,' I replied, turning to the Queen, and ignoring the presence of the herald.

" ' Thou art alive,' continued Didoné.

" ' By thy grace alone do I live, Lady.'

" ' Thy pale hide still covers thee,' burst in Limpopo ; ' thy naked quivering nerves are not yet powdered with the chili-dust.'

" ' I am still unskinned, eternal star, and as yet my nerves are unpeppered,' I replied, continuing to address myself to Didoné, and assuming an appearance of calmness, though I inwardly shuddered at the horrors that awaited me.

" ' Ah ! but not for long, not for long,' screamed the herald, in a rising burst of rage ; ' the flaying knives are a-sharpening, and the yellow chilis are crackling in the pestle. Dost thou hear me, O deaf adder of the swamp ? '

" Didoné visibly trembled, but she repeated,—

" ' Dost thou hear ? '

" ' I hear, sweet gleamer of the night,' I answered, with an air of unconcern.

" ' And dost thou know the fate in store for thee when thy vile casing hath gone, and thy writhing nerves are tortured into madness ? ' thundered Limpopo.

" ' I know not, orb of day. I am a stranger in thy happy realm,' said I, regarding Didoné with a smile.

" ' The royal emmets cry for thy living blood,' gasped my enemy, in a voice hoarse and almost inarticulate with fury.

" ' But now, even now, thou canst escape,' said Didoné, regarding me anxiously; ' even now thy life is thine if thou sendest me the rose.'

" For a moment I hesitated; then a reckless feeling of defiance possessed me ; they had bullied me till I was stubborn and prepared for resistance to the death. Had they gone another way to work I might have surrendered, but, as it was, I replied,—

" ' Thy mercy, exquisite scintilla of high heaven, is far beyond my poor deserts. I am unworthy to receive the honour of thy hand,' and drawing my pipe from my pocket I lighted it deliberately and, placing myself at ease upon the skins, proceeded to smoke as though I were alone.

" My words, coupled with this rude show of indifference, seemed to provoke the Queen to sudden madness. The gold box that she carried contained the bodies of the hairy variety of the red spider pounded into a paste—a poison of which the slightest touch entails a lingering death of the most hideous agony. Inserting the point of her dagger into the mixture, she rose to her feet and rushed towards me, saying :—' Flames consume my soul. Thy heart's blood shall quench them,' but, catching her foot in her long robe, she stumbled, and would have fallen had I not caught her in my arms. Carefully re-seating her upon her throne, I respectfully handed her the dagger and the gold box, both of which had fallen on the ground ; I then resumed my place upon the otter-skins.

" During this scene her attendants had remained immobile, Limpopo alone giving vent to his feelings by a savage yell. The soldiers had apparently been directed not to move hand or foot, except at the Queen's command. For a moment Didoné sat gazing fixedly on the ground, her face flushing and her bosom heaving with excitement, her fingers twitching around the dagger, and her foot passionately beating the floor. I fully expected to see the attack repeated. I was then ignorant of the contents of the gold box—though I afterwards received instruction on this point from Limpopo—and should have considered myself fortunate if I had been despatched then and there, for in comparison with the revolting atrocities that were preparing for me, death by the dagger would have been merciful. Didoné's anger, however, gave place to other emotions, and suddenly covering her face with her veil she rose and hurriedly left the cottage, followed by her body-guard and the herald.

"A week passed without either any change in the method of my captivity or the slightest alleviation of its rigour. On the morning of the eighth day Limpopo zealously escorted me, heavily ironed and closely guarded, to the audience-hall. The vast chamber was thronged with hostile faces, for the news of my insulting behaviour to the Queen had excited universal indignation, and there were few men present who would not have thought themselves privileged to be allowed a few minutes' loose lance-practice on my unhappy body. Didoné sat enthroned upon the daïs, closely veiled as on the day when I first beheld her, and at the further end of the hall, confronting the Queen, was a very remarkable-looking old man. His nose was hooked like the beak of a vulture;

his forehead was low and very protuberant, his small black eyes gleamed stern and menacing beneath his shaggy eyebrows; a fell of curly white hair hung half down his back; and a snowy beard descended to his knees. He was enthroned upon a massive silver chair, and by his side stood a tall youth, supporting an enormous book bound with crocodile-skin and fastened with heavy gold clasps. The old man was no other than Johannes Tagazze, or Terrible John, Chief Judge of Abyssinia; a man who revelled in cruelty, and exhausted his ingenuity in devising the grossest barbarities for his victims, while his blind hatred for the white race bordered upon madness. This was the man whom Limpopo had persuaded Didoné in the first frenzy of her anger to summon from Magdala in order to pronounce my doom. The book by his side was the volume of the law; it was written in the *Lisana Matzhaf*, or clerical language, and as I did not understand this obsolete tongue, the old man translated what he read into Tigrani.

"On my arrival in the hall, I was placed in a sort of raised pen in the centre, facing the Judge, who, after glancing towards Didoné, as though formally asking leave to begin, addressed me as follows :—

" 'Listen, O man doomed to death. Listen to the fate assigned by the laws of Adowa to the

R

wretch that scorns the hand of royalty,' and the old tyrant began to read from the volume, emphasizing with an unctuous relish every phrase of more than ordinarily cruel import. I need not recapitulate the monstrous horrors to which he condemned me ; suffice it to say that the terrors announced by Limpopo formed but a small part of the agonies allotted to me by the law. My execution, if I lived so long, was to last three weeks ! The sentence concluded with the words : ' And thy hair shall be spun into a mat for the royal feet, and thy skin shall be formed into slippers.'

"He closed the book with a snap, and having glared pitilessly at me for a few seconds, turned to the Queen and inquired when she would wish the tortures to commence. She hesitated for a moment, and then in a faltering tone murmured :—

" ' Great Father of Pain, thy words are as the merciful dew that falls on the valleys of Ras Dashan, but the law of Habesh is above us all, and by the law alone must we proceed.'

" ' And have I not expounded the law ? ' snarled Johannes, regarding the Queen malevolently. ' Am I not the Chief Interpreter thereof ? What is it that the Royal Lustre would alter or amend ? '

" ' Doth not the law, O tender Tagazze, enjoin

upon us heed, lest we shed the royal blood?' inquired Didoné.

" 'Aye, ye may find it so written in the third verse of the second chapter,' said Tagazze, addressing the crowd of upturned startled faces, 'Her Brilliancy hath learnt it aright, whosoever may have been her prompter,' and he glanced ominously at those on the daïs.

" '*My* blood, O gentle Johannes, mingles with thy captive's. He and I are knit together by the scarlet bond.'

" The Judge's cruel features, which during this short passage had set like iron, now relaxed into a ferocious smile.

" 'Ye are coupled in the living link? Say ye so? 'Tis true, Scintilla, that thy blood must not be shed. No, the doomed slave may not be flayed, neither may the emmets drain him, but he shall nathless perish in the flame,' and waving his gaunt hand towards me, he cried, 'Bear him to the Judge's pit! He kindleth to-morrow at daybreak.'

" At these words my guards, closing round me, conducted me towards a low black-curtained door at the side of the hall.

" 'Hold!' commanded Didoné, her musical voice ringing like a clarion. 'Cast him not into thy pit; Johannes; replace him in the lodge.'

R 2

" ' To the pit ! ' thundered Terrible John, rising from his seat in fury.

" ' To the lodge!' cried Didoné, and in obedience to her signal some of the Royal Guards attempted to break through the iron hedge that environed me.

" ' Ha ! A rescue of the Judge's captive ! ' roared Limpopo, brandishing his spear. ' Who is for Johannes ? '

" ' Who is for Didoné ? ' shrieked the Queen, springing to her feet, and throwing off her veil.

" Some twenty of her immediate followers ranged themselves behind Didoné ; but, with this exception, the entire assembly gathered round Terrible John, who, still standing rigid as an angry cobra, waved his hand in triumph, and vociferated,—

" ' To the pit with the dog ! Away ! '

" The odds were so fearfully against Didoné that any further attempt to save me at that juncture would have resulted only in the immediate massacre of her adherents, and amid much uproar and confusion I was dragged through the side porch, and thrust into a loathsome cavity without light, and with but little air.

" I spent the night in reflecting upon the horror of my position. As I told myself that but eight hours lay between me and an excruciating death,

I asked myself whether I had not been a madman to repel the advances of the Queen. Had I consented, I should at this moment have been the most powerful man in Tigré, Limpopo would have been but a worm in my path, and I might have defied even Johannes Tagazze. Why did I want to go back to Aden? Had there not been instances of white kings ruling dark races? Didoné was a lovely woman, an intelligent and affectionate companion, and there was no doubt of the depth of her love for me. What an insensate fool, what a maniac I had been !

" Before daybreak on the following morning the mouth of my den was opened and I was led forth to my death. We passed through the audience-chamber, which, now silent and deserted, presented a marked contrast to the angry tumult of the previous day. Through the hall they led me, out into the courtyard and under the mighty gateway into the great park. Early though the hour, the park was thronged with an eager multitude, for under the clement rule of Didoné the burning of a living man was a rare and unique spectacle. In the centre of the park was a black mound, on which had been erected a heavy wooden post furnished with chains and straps, and near at hand lay an abundance of brushwood and faggots.

At a convenient distance from the stake sat the Chief Judge in a silken litter borne upon men's shoulders; and among the faggots stood Limpopo, furnished with an enormous torch, which he was in the act of lighting. In the twinkling of an eye I was bound hand and foot to the stake, with the brushwood and faggots piled around me. Terrible John, seeing that everything was ready, then gave the order to light the pile.

" Had Limpopo obeyed the command at once, nothing could have saved me; but my enemy wished to prolong his enjoyment of the scene, and, approaching me, said in a voice of mock humility, as he made an exaggerated reverence:—

. " ' How fareth my lord the husband of the Queen ? Hath he any orders for his slave ? Doth he go to the chase to-day ? or will he ride his palfrey in the park ? What ! neither ? Then, perchance, my lord abideth in the palace, and will eat of the fat and drink of the sweet, and listen to music in the bower ? Ah ! dread lord, speak to thy humble slave, or he will fear he hath aroused thy grave displeasure. Maybe poor Limpopo findeth no favour in his master's sight, and his lord will order the insolent Chamberlain to be scourged or tormented of the emmets. What ! silent still ? Nay, then, it must be the cold of the early morning that distresseth my liege and master. This we will straightway alleviate, and he shall have warmth—aye, warmth for bone and blood, warmth for heart and brain, warmth that shall cherish and comfort and delight;' and grinning malignantly, he slowly advanced the torch towards the brushwood.

"While Limpopo was speaking I, from my elevated position, had observed, over the heads of the crowd, a party of horsemen emerging from the palace-gates. The gaze of the spectators was fixed on me, and the riders approached unperceived. Suddenly their pace was quickened, and they came down upon us at full gallop. They were headed by Didoné, who, clothed from head to foot in gleaming armour, seemed like some glorious young Amazon leading her legions to the war. At the sound of the approaching hoofs the crowd fell back, leaving a clear space round the pyre. In another moment the faggots were scattered in all directions, the thongs that bound me to the stake were cut, and I found myself, mounted on a spare horse, forcing my way through the yielding crowd, with Didoné riding at my side. Limpopo, who vainly attempted to arrest our progress, was struck down and trampled, I trust to death, beneath the hoofs of the horses. Once clear of the throng we increased our pace. We flew through the park-gates and, leaving Axum behind us, struck across the great plain to the southward. We rode hard for about three miles, and then proceeded more leisurely; this afforded me my first opportunity of exchanging a word with Didoné. She was in the highest spirits, and cried joyously :—

" ' Once again I have foiled Tagazze. They can never catch us now. They will find their horses useless, for I caused leaves of the *tromo* to be placed in the water-troughs last night.'

" She then told me how she had at first thought to frighten me into the fulfilment of our betrothal, but finding me obdurate, she had, in the brief madness of her anger, allowed Limpopo to persuade her to send for Terrible John. She had no sooner sent for the old ruffian than she regretted what she had done; but the call was irrevocable, and Johannes travelled day and night to perform the congenial task. After his arrival affairs had altogether escaped her guidance, and it was only by such a desperate act as this that she could save me from Tagazze's truculence. Her plan now was to make for Magdala, where her Uncle Lijkasa, whom we call Theodore, would protect her from the vengeance of the Judge.

Johannes, I must tell you, was, after the Emperor, all-powerful in matters connected with the administration of the law, and Didoné, by robbing him of his victim, had incurred the direst penalties. She had once before offended him in the same way—in the matter of old Guldu—and it was only by the direct interposition of her uncle that she escaped dethronement. As for me, and she smiled significantly, if I obeyed her in everything, my safety was assured.

" Although we felt secure against pursuit, we pushed on briskly through the broken country lying between Axum and Magdala, for Didoné was anxious to explain matters to her uncle in her own way before he · could receive Tagazze's version, which would certainly be despatched by the swiftest runner in Axum. On the third day we fell in with Theodore, who, accompanied by a small company of horse, was reconnoitring the country to the north of Magdala. The Emperor's reception of his niece was affectionate, but on me he looked coldly.

" ' Whence the captive of thy spear?' he inquired.

" ' He is no prisoner of war.'

" ' What then?'

" ' He is bondsman to my beauty,' laughed the girl.

" The Negus frowned at the jest, and bid me fall
to the rear; then, with Didoné by his side, he placed
himself at the head of the combined cavalcade and
proceeded at a canter towards the great rock-
fortress that towered dark and grim against the
evening sky.

" On arriving at Magdala we drew up in the great
square, and the Negus, having given some directions in an undertone to an attendant, beckoned to
Didoné, and led the way to the palace, leaving me
surrounded by the soldiers. As he turned to go
the Princess caught him by the robe, and, pointing
to me, said in a firm voice :—

" ' Uncle, he also must accompany thee.'

" ' Nay, he goeth to the nether pit ; I have scores
such as he in duress.'

" ' Wouldst thou disgrace thus thy niece's husband?'

" ' What ! thy husband, Didoné, and I not told ?
Why, girl, I did not hear even of thy rose-binding.'

" ' We are not yet bound by the rose, but we are
plighted in the scarlet.'

" ' Pshaw ! that Obi rite of ancient days is nought.
A royal hand can solve the red knot, and I, the
Negus, do it.'

" ' Hold ! not even the Negus Negest (king of
kings) can break the link we forged in Axum.'

" 'What hast thou done, thou wilful girl, that Lijkasa cannot reverse? Who forged thy link?'

" ' Twas Prester John himself, Lijkasa, his the spear-point that shed our blood, his the zone that bound our arms, and his the hand that blessed our bridal.'

" Theodore's swarthy face grew black with passion, and his words burst forth like a torrent :

" ' Thou tampering ghoul ! thou naughty hyena ! the hermit thou hast suborned shall blaze for this. He hath betrayed his trust. Hast thou not heard it said that when the bones of Prester John are moved the Empire falls? Ah! old Guldu blazeth high ; he smoketh black. When the red soldiers shall have fled the land I haste to Axum, and Guldu becometh a cinder.'

" Impulsive as a child, the plaything of his own emotions, and swayed like a feather in the wind by every passing thought, Theodore's most striking characteristic was his sudden change of mood. This reference to the red soldiers served to divert his ideas into a new channel, and turning to the men around me, he cried :—

" ' Bring hither the Axum Queen's pet antelope that I may see him closer.'

" When I was brought before him he gazed at me steadfastly, muttering to himself the while. I could not catch what he was saying, but I heard him twice repeat the words 'red soldiers, knowledge, and counsel.' Suddenly breaking off he bid me accompany him and Didoné into the banqueting chamber, where we found food and wine awaiting us. As the meal proceeded we conversed in Tigrani. He now laughed at the prophecy he had quoted to Didoné, but asked many questions touching the strength of our army and the valour of our troops, and was extremely anxious to discover the favourite ruses of our Generals. With each course he grew more friendly, and when we rose from the repast he took me aside and promised that as soon as the red soldiers had quitted the country he would permit Didoné to accept the rose, after which our nuptials were to be celebrated with unusual splendour, under his immediate superintendence. The red soldiers referred to by the Negus were Sir Robert Napier's troops, then within a few marches of Magdala.

"Theodore's regard for me grew stronger every day, and by the end of the week he loved me like a brother. He would never ride out without having me as his companion, and he would spend hours strolling round the ramparts with his arm locked in mine. After dinner we always played chess, while Didoné sang us some wild tale of the brave days of old. But all this time the British Army was advancing, and as it drew near his capital Theodore disclosed a restlessness and anxiety which grew hour by hour more painfully acute, and when the cloud of dust that hung over our advance guard was seen from the watch-tower he summoned me to join his chiefs in consultation. Outside the council-chamber were seated seven wild-looking, travel-stained men, with unkempt hair and fantastic garments. These were seven very eminent soothsayers, whom he had gathered from distant quarters of the Empire to read the issue of the coming strife. As I entered the room, Theodore was giving an order, with his customary impetuosity, to one of the attendant chiefs, and, turning to me, he said that as Sir Robert Napier had opened fire upon him he had ordered the immediate execution of all the British prisoners. I earnestly begged him not to carry out this intention until we had fully discussed the matter. I had already employed my influence with him to secure better treatment for the prisoners during their captivity, and my power over him was now so great that in the space of a quarter of an hour I succeeded, not only in getting the order for the execution cancelled, but in obtaining an edict for a general release. I then left the assembly in order to see that the warrant of manumission was duly obeyed, and as I opened the door to go, the Negus called in the soothsayers.

"An hour later Didoné sought me out. 'Terrible things are happening,' she cried. 'The soothsayers have divined what passed in Guldu's cave, and have foretold my uncle's defeat and dishonour. The warriors are fleeing from him as from one doomed to destruction, and barely a hundred spearmen remain to defend the fortress. Lijkasa has vowed that your countrymen shall enter the royal stronghold only over his dead body. The red soldiers even now are moving towards the hill, and the Negus has gone to the outer gate that he may meet his death.'

"Bidding Didoné remain under cover, I ran to the ramparts, and could perceive our advancing skirmishers covering a large body of troops marching in the direction of the rock. Beyond the attacking force were the white tents that marked the British encampment.

"As I approached the great gate, I heard, amid the whistling of the bullets that were now flying in all directions, the sharp ring of a pistol-shot, and, turning into the gateway, I stood by the prostrate body of the King. I was just a minute too late to save him; all assistance was now in vain. He was stone dead, and had clearly fallen by his own hand.

" I hastened to break the news to Didoné ; but after wandering here and there through the now nearly deserted fortress without finding her, I returned to the ramparts in order to observe the advance of the British column. The skirmishers had now reached the base of the rock and were about to mount the acclivity. As I gazed with admiration at the steady order of their ascent a little hand was laid lightly on my shoulder. I turned and beheld Didoné. She was dressed from head to foot in delicate chain-mail, as on the day she rescued me from Tagazze, only now she wore on her head a bright steel cap embossed with silver knobs and adorned with a marabout feather : behind her were grouped some fifty horsemen. Addressing me in her low, melodious voice, she said :—

" ' Lijkasa, alas ! is dead ; I am now Empress of Abyssinia and mistress of my fate. In half an hour '—and she pointed to the soldiers toiling up the rock—' your countrymen will be dominant here, and I, if I remain, shall be as a snared bird in your hands. Tell me, B'langi ' (that was her rendering of my name), ' tell me, by thy Sacred One, wilt thou, if I yield myself—say, wilt thou be kind and true to me, wilt thou give me the rose and live with me, beloved and loving, in the bond ? '

" I was silent. What reply could I make to this appeal?

" ' These warriors,' she continued, as she pointed to the horsemen, ' have hailed me Empress of Ethiopia and Queen of Abyssinia. They urge me to fly to the shores of Lake Tzana, there to rule over what remains of my uncle's empire. My reason would have me depart; but, ah ! my heart weeps and cries no. Tell me, B'langi, beloved, shall I go or stay ? '

" I clapsed her in my arms, and as I strained her to my heart I whispered : ' Didoné, sweetest and dearest of women, I love thee too well to bid thee tarry.'

" She tore herself from my embrace, and, leaping on her horse, uttered a few rapid words to her attendants, who shouted and waved their lances in jubilation; then, wheeling about, they made their clever horses jump in single file from the ramparts to a grass-covered ledge of rock a few feet below, whence they slid and crept laboriously from shelf to shelf along some path known only to the riders, until they reached the plain. Didoné was the last to descend. As she reined in her beautiful black barb on the broad rampart, she turned and regarded me with a dreamy expression of loving despair, then the old smile played for a moment over her lips, and she murmured in Abyssinian: 'Farewell, my beloved, farewell to thee for ever.'

"She then put her horse to the leap and followed her escort down the rock.

"Shortly after Didoné's departure I admitted our troops into the fortress, but I felt that as yet I had no further concern with them. Returning to the battlements, I sat watching the little knot of cavalry as it grew smaller in the distance until it was lost to view. For a moment there gleamed out of the haze on the horizon what seemed to be a star; it was the sunlight on Didoné's helm. As it vanished in the mist my romance ended, and the world of prosaic work again received me.

"Descending from the ramparts, I sought the General, and made a full confession of my escapade, of course not forgetting to recount how I had been instrumental in saving the lives of the prisoners. The narrative created much interest at head-quarters, and the good-hearted chief not only forgave me for my shameless breach of discipline but offered to mention my name in despatches. This distinction, however, I respectfully but firmly

s

declined, and I begged as a personal favour that the account of my adventures might go no further than the Head-Quarter Staff, lest it should bring poor Didoné's name into notoriety, and induce romantic subalterns to desert their posts and roam about Abyssinia hunting for Princesses."

THE WHITE SOWAR.

——o——

A CHANGE had come over Colonel Bowlong.
During the past six weeks his altered demeanour
had occasioned us increasing anxiety, not un-
mingled with alarm; his once cheery greeting had
given place to a cold salute; his eye no longer
twinkled with the old mirth-provoking light; and
his deep, kindly laugh, that made the laughter of
others flow in responsive sympathy, was now but
seldom heard. His rich fund of anecdote seemed
to be exhausted; his talk at mess wore an
unfamiliar terseness that in a man made up of
less genial elements would have been resented as
morose; even the sallies of the vivacious Snapper
failed to rouse him from his lethargy; and in the
verandah, so long the forum of his eloquence, he
would sit in the autocratic seclusion of a gloomy
silence until he had consumed his favourite
cheroot of " Thompson's muster," and then, rising
abruptly with an abstracted nod, and a curt " good-

night " to his nearest neighbour, he would call for his carriage, and go home. Was the old man ill? Was our deeply-valued friend beginning to droop under the cold eye of the pale destroyer, who, with impartial foot, kicks open the door alike of Colonel and Cornet, and summons the shivering occupant to join one of old Charon's unpopular boating parties on the darkling mystic river? Could it be that we were about to lose our old Chief?

One evening at mess—how well each detail of that night comes back to my memory—after striving ineffectually to keep up the leaden ball of artificial gaiety, we lapsed into silence. There was upon us the sense of an impending sorrow, and I for one felt small talk impossible.

" Butler, champagne to every one." It was the Colonel's voice, but so unfamiliar was the tone, so solemn was it, and so sad, that all present started with surprise. When the wine had gone round, Colonel Bowlong rose to his feet, and after one or two husky coughs spoke as follows: " Gentlemen,—I mean, my very dear fellows, that confounded White Sowar——"

But before I proceed with the Colonel's speech I must give the story of this same White Sowar, as our old friend told it in the days when his heart was light. It ran thus:—

"On returning to India after the Abyssinian expedition, I took sixty days' privilege-leave, and went shooting in the Jhoot jungles. I had not been in those parts since I was a griffin, and I was amused to find that the recollection of my youthful exploits was still fresh in the minds of the people. Indeed, I fancy that even now they talk of the boy that killed the 'Demon.' On my arrival at Nubli, a small village at the foot of the Teltu Hills, I found the villagers in a state of the wildest excitement of joy at my advent; the entire hamlet turned out to greet me with tom-toms and garlands and fruit. 'What's it all about?' I asked, as the head-man put a wreath of jasmine round my neck.

"'All the world is saying,' replied the old man, gleefully, 'that the nourisher of the poor has come to rid us of the "White Sowar" as in days of old he freed us from the "Jhoot Demon."'

"'The White Sowar!' I exclaimed, 'and who the dickens may *he* be?' Whereupon the entire crowd began to speak at once with much dramatic gesticulation, and it was not without considerable difficulty that I came to understand that a white man, well armed and marvellously mounted, had taken up his abode in the heart of the forest, whence he levied blackmail on the neighbourhood.

for a radius of five-and-twenty miles. Of course this information did not come to me precisely in the above form; the materials from which I gathered it were of a far more poetical nature. According to my informants, the country had, for the last eighteen months or so, fallen under the sway of a malignant spirit, a dauntless white devil of infinite power and unappeasable malevolence, who, mounted on a winged horse, swept like the angel of death over the face of the land, leaving behind him nothing but blood and ashes.

"That night my runner was stopped, and next morning I had no bread for breakfast. I now saw that the matter was serious, and must be attended to without delay, so I included the robber in the list of wild animals for whose *khubber** I offered a reward. My rate was five rupees for news of a bison, ten for a tiger, and fifteen for the White Sowar. A week passed, and reports of his depredations came in from all quarters, but the intelligence received told me only where he had been last heard of, not where he was now to be found. One evening, however, as I was returning from shooting, I was accosted by a hairy old Bhil, in appearance not unlike a venerable chimpanzee, who reported that he had seen the

* News.

'Sowar devil' taking post in a thicket near the cart-track that ran through the jungle from Kandalur to Nubli. The rascal was again lying in wait for my runner; he evidently liked baker's bread. Following the Bhil, and bidding my gun-bearer keep close, I dived into the jungle, and proceeded as rapidly as the wait-a-bit thorns would permit. We tore our way through the bushes for about two miles, and just as the sun was setting I saw the white cart-track gleaming between the stems of the sâl-trees. At that moment, my guide suddenly crouched behind a bush, signalling to me to do the same. He then extended a bony first finger to his front, and sat breathless, staring, and rigid—a perfect picture of a forest animal in the presence of supreme and immediate peril from which it cannot flee. In the shadow of the foliage, some fifty yards away, I saw a horseman, dressed like an Australian bushranger, and armed with a cavalry carbine that he rested dragoon-fashion on his thigh. Both man and horse were perfectly still, and it was clear that our approach had been unobserved. I turned for my rifle, but my gun-bearer was nowhere to be seen! At this juncture I heard the jingle of the bells which told me that my weekly supply of bread and other creature comforts was at hand, and in a minute or two more would be in the grasp of the spoiler. The Bhil's sole weapon was a bow-and-arrow; I silently relieved him of his artillery and awaited the event. Nearer and nearer rang the bells, and the bearer, going at a good swinging trot, suddenly came into view round the corner of the road.

" ' *Halt!* ' shouted the horseman, as he wheeled his charger into the centre of the path and covered the runner with his carbine. The terrified cossid took in the situation at a glance: he waited for no further manifestation, but, with a cry of alarm, threw down his burden and dived like a deer into the jungle. The robber dismounted and began leisurely to rifle the bags; he regarded the bread approvingly, and seemed well pleased at the appearance of a bottle of Irish whiskey; but what delighted him most of all was a box of Manilla cigars, which he at once broke open and the contents of which he proceeded to sample. Having tied up his spoil he remounted. It was a trying moment. I felt that the contest would be altogether unequal, but hang me if I could let him go with all the honours of war. So I stepped from my concealment and cried, as I drew the arrow to the head,—

" ' Surrender, or you are a dead man ! '

. " He looked at me for an instant with amazement, but when he realized that I was threatening him with a bow-and-arrow he laughed with such uncontrollable violence that his lately lighted cigar fell from his mouth. He then raised his carbine, but before he could take aim I loosed the arrow. It struck him somewhere in the chest, and as it pierced him he reeled and nearly let his weapon fall, but recovering himself by a manful effort he turned his horse, and swaying from side to side, galloped madly up the road. He was evidently hard hit, and feeling himself, even with his superior weapon, altogether overmatched, he was making with the instinct of a wounded animal for his lair. The sun had now disappeared and pursuit that night was out of the question, but, sending for dogs and trackers, I prepared to run the prey to earth in the morning.

"Next day, at daybreak, I found my tents surrounded by an animated crowd of shikaris, trackers, and villagers, armed with spears, lathies, bows-and-arrows, and rusty matchlocks. There were also some Bhils leading knowing-looking dogs tied in couples ; and the entire assembly was frantic with the hope that the horseman-fiend had seen the dawn of his last day. Before starting, I strictly forbade a shot to be fired or a blow to be struck without my orders. The business of the natives was to track, mine either to capture or to kill, as circumstances might dictate. I had resolved, however, that I would take the freebooter alive.

"Laying on the dogs at the spot where the robber had received his wound, we were led along the Nubli road for about a mile, when the trail turned sharply to the left, taking the direction of the Teltu Hills. This range, which consisted of a series of elevations covered with the densest jungle, and rising in terraces, one above the other, contained the most inaccessible recesses of the Great Jhoot. Pursuit now became slower; now and then a tracker would come to me with a leaf or a blade of grass bearing a spot of blood, and I confess that as I viewed these signs of successful shikar, I recoiled from the idea that I was pursuing my own countryman as though he were a wounded roebuck. The track at last led us to where a magnificent waterfall flashed and thundered down the mountain-side. The torrent was both wide and deep; black jagged rocks reared their heads in mid-stream; the banks were stony and precipitous, and here both hound and tracker paused. It was evident to all present that the fugitive had leapt the fall. In any circumstances it would have been a gallant feat, but performed in the twilight and by a wounded man it was a

splendid achievement. It forcibly reminded me
of the grand reckless horsemanship of the old
Pandours, and I began to feel a reluctant
admiration for this fearless solitary lord of the
wilderness whom I was hunting, possibly to
death. Acting on the impulse of the moment,
I summarily dismissed my rabble rout, retaining
only one veteran shikari, whose skill in taking
up the trail appeared to me to be more in
the nature of inspiration than of reason, and
with Loobu as my sole companion I forded the
foaming stream some hundred yards lower down,
resuming the track where the starred and
splintered rock showed that the horse had landed.
After more than two hours' laborious climb, we
found ourselves on a little grassy plateau that
crested the highest hill of the series; in our front
frowned a large rocky cave, and a clear stream of
sparkling water flowed through a little lawn. Two
stately tamarind-trees shaded the entrance to the
cavern, and the place altogether formed a most
perfect sylvan hermitage. How its European occupant ever discovered it, passes my comprehension.
My guide, telling me to lie quiet behind a clump of
pampas-grass, wriggled, snake-like, to the cave
and reconnoitred. After a brief inspection he
returned, carrying something which he handed to

me with a grave smile. It was the Bhil's arrow
stained with blood from point to feather. Beyond
a doubt we had run the robber to earth ; the task
now was to draw him. Handing my rifle to the
old man, I cocked my revolver and we entered the
cave together. As we crossed the threshold, a shot
rang out from the interior and a bullet whistled
between us; the explosion lighted up the cavern,
and I could see, lying on a heap of straw at the
far end of the recess, the wounded outlaw, in the
act of exchanging his carbine for a pistol. Before
he could fire a second shot I had closed with him,
and in his enfeebled state there was no great
difficulty in overpowering him. Loobu having
struck a light, I found that we were in a large rocky
cavity, spacious enough to afford shelter for half a
dozen men and horses. Scattered around were
the proceeds of many a daring raid—food, clothes,
arms, and jewellery lay about in careless pro-
fusion. In one corner stood the horse, a fine
animal with B. 23 still perceptible on its near fore.

" ' Aha ! my friend,' said I, ' so you have been
helping yourself from a cavalry stable.'

" ' Bowlong,' said the wounded man, faintly,
' you wouldn't smash an old Pandour ? '

" ' *An old Pandour !* You an old Pan ! Why,
who in the name of wonder are you ? ' I cried.

"'Don't you remember Heatherstone—"Wild Heather"? I recognized you in the jungle yesterday. I never meant to shoot you. You were precious quick, though, with your blessed bow. Always good at that, weren't you, old man?'

"I held the torch to his face. Yes, sure enough, it was Heatherstone, once cornet in my own troop, the brightest and cheeriest young fellow I had ever met. Broken by court-martial for cheeking the Colonel on parade—touch of the sun you know—and for trying to cut down the Adjutant when that officer demanded his sword, he had, on the night of his sentence, taken the best horse in the Regiment and disappeared; he had been searched for far and wide without the discovery of sign or trace of him. Since then, he had lived the life of a solitary man-brute, pitiless and ravening, 'red in tooth and claw' as, as—the sportsman says. Well, of course, I ought to have handed him over to the authorities and have had him transported or hanged, for I fear there was but little doubt that he had more than once taken life in his forays. But I did not do my duty. I tended him carefully till he was well. Loobu, prompted thereto by liberal largess, kept the secret with exemplary fidelity, and in the course of a month or two I got poor Heatherstone safely out of the country. I heard that shortly after his return to England he tumbled into an enormous fortune."

That was the story of the White Sowar—I will now resume my account of the Colonel's speech.

" That confounded White Sowar, Heatherstone you know, has lost the number of his mess—broke his neck hunting—and has left me twenty lakhs. His lawyers write to say that there is a little place in the Shires, shooting estate in Scotland, fine castle in Cadiz, steam-yacht, horses, carriages, and I don't know what, all mine. Worst of it is, I must go home at once and look after 'em. I wouldn't tell you fellows about it till I had made sure, in case I piled it up too high—couldn't do that, you know—couldn't do that. But it's all cut and dried, and I'm to hand over charge of the Regiment to the Major here to-morrow, and then—I'm off for ever."

At this point the speaker became so deeply affected that he might have been announcing his irreparable ruin instead of describing a splendid inheritance. But by an effort he controlled himself, and proposed the health and prosperity of the Regiment, with the usual honours. Bewildered, we performed the function.

" Three cheers for Marmaduke Bowlong, kindest of 'friends and best of Colonels," shouted the

Major, rising to his feet, and *then* we made the
roof ring and the glasses caper. When the cheer-
ing had a bit subsided the Major delivered such
a neat little speech that no room was left for
doubt that he had all the time been in the
Colonel's confidence and had been duly given the
' office '; and then we cheered again until we had
to desist from sheer exhaustion, and all the time
the dear old Chief sat with his handkerchief to
his face crying like a child. Later on we escorted
him home, and next morning saw him safe off on
his journey to Bombay.

*   *   *   *   *

When Colonel Bowlong's Indian friends go to
England they receive no warmer welcome from
even the nearest and dearest of their kin than that
which is extended to them by the good old Colonel.
All of us in the Regiment have spent many happy
weeks at his little place in the Shires, but, strange
to say, I never met any one who had stayed either
at the Scotch shooting-box or at the Spanish
castle. The Colonel says that he finds the climate
of Ayrshire a trifle too cold for him, and that of
Andalucia just a degree too warm.

THE END.

www.ingramcontent.com/pod-product-compliance
Lightning Source LLC
Chambersburg PA
CBHW021056030726
47496CB00006B/1869